I0769469

WHISPERS
IN THE
DARK

A.E. FAULKNER

CONTENTS

Open House

"Another Sunday, another open house," Jean huffs, pushing the white lace curtain aside to get a clearer view of the yellow split-level home that seems to be a revolving door for new neighbors.

"So what?" Hal asks without looking up from his newspaper. "It's none of our business."

"But it *is* our business." She crosses her arms and looks from Hal, who's still seated at the table, to the view just past her window. "We have to live two houses down from whatever stranger moves in next. We have to deal with the noise from the moving trucks and construction people they hire to build an addition or replace the roof. Then a year later, it happens all over again."

Hal stands and delivers his empty coffee mug to the sink before joining her at the window. He peers out over her wispy fluff of blond hair. "Doesn't even feel worth trying to get to know them anymore. By the time you get used to seeing them around, they're packing up and then all of a sudden the house is empty and they're just gone."

"Have you noticed," Jean asks, "that it's always the same realtor? How is that even possible? How many hundreds of realtors show houses in this area? How has this one person managed to always sell the same house?"

"You sure?" Hal asks, glancing at the living room. "Maybe it's one agency or something but different agents."

"No, it's always the same person. Elena Tarasenko. I'd recognize her anywhere. Her picture's always plastered across the 'for sale' sign, her face painted with eye shadow, blush and lipstick. The huge, gaudy sign makes our street look like we have a permanent yard sale or something. I just know something's fishy over there!" Jean wrings her hands in frustration, her cheeks flushing a deeper shade of crimson with each word.

"You're making too much out of this. Who cares about the realtor, or the house?" Hal turns and shuffles into the living room. The television clicks on and the familiar pre-game music plays, announcing the start of a football match-up.

Well, that's it, Jean thinks to herself. *He may not believe me, but I'm right. I'm going over there. Maybe I can help Elena weed out people who aren't serious about staying.* This is a nice neighborhood. Everyone else has managed to stay living here for decades, passing their homes down through generations of family members. But that one house has had three different owners in the last five years. It makes it seem like something is wrong with this street. If this keeps up, it could drive down home values.

Jean stomps over to the table and collects the lunch dishes. She stacks them neatly in the sink. "I'm going to check out the open house," she calls. "I'll be back in a bit."

"Uh-huh," Hal mutters, not taking his eyes off the television.

Jean strides down the sidewalk, making a beeline for the front door. She grasps the handle, twists it and barges inside. An earthy smell tickles her nose, as if a plant was knocked over nearby. She scans the sparse entranceway, noting no living greens. A narrow mahogany table is nestled beside the door, staged with random knickknacks and a basket for the prospective homeowner to drop their keys inside. Beside it, a sleek glass vase cradles stick-straight white tulips. Jean pinches a smooth petal between her fingers – it's silk. Of course, everything here is probably fake, just for show, she thinks.

"Hello!" The realtor barrels to the door, her slender fingers with perfectly manicured nails extend toward Jean for a firm handshake. "I'm Elena. Thanks for coming. Can I show you around or answer any questions?"

Jean purses her lips. There's only one question on her mind and she has nothing to lose by asking it.

"Yes, actually, I'm one of the neighbors and I've noticed that this house is for sale . . . a lot. It seems like it's for sale more than it's actually lived in." Jean holds her tongue, waiting for Elena's reaction.

Elena's ruby red lips pull into a tight smile. "Well, this home has passed through a few different families in recent years, but it's only because they all had wonderful opportunities come up that they just couldn't pass up."

"Opportunities? It's not like they sold it right away and someone bought it up for millions of dollars. If that was the case, there wouldn't be so many open houses." Jean crosses her arms and cocks her head to the side. She's tired of this revolving door of neighbors and the realtor might as well know it.

"Well . . . ," Elena says, gently placing her palm on Jean's elbow. "Why don't I show you what makes this house so special? Have you ever toured it?"

"No, I haven't," Jean says, shrugging away from Elena's touch.

"Then come with me." Elena turns her back on Jean and throws a hand over her shoulder in a "this way" gesture.

"Fine." Jean doesn't bother to hide her lack of enthusiasm. She wants an answer. A simple answer, not a tour. But if this is what it takes to get to the bottom of anything, she can waste a few minutes oohing and ahhing over closet storage and built-in bookshelves, or whatever this place has that makes people want to buy it, even if they don't stay.

Elena leads her to the kitchen, which is nothing special. The sparkling pearl countertop and pristine white cabinets are spacious. The wooden dining table with four sets of navy fabric placemats and oversized white napkins folded like little chef's hats is inviting, but Jean isn't impressed. It's not much different from her kitchen's layout. Stainless steel appliances stand at the ready, just waiting for someone to use them. Big deal, she thinks, she has those too.

When Elena pulls open one of the three doors within the space, Jean assumes she's about to see a pantry that would make any cook envious. Unable to hide her confusion, her eyes narrow when she realizes it's a door to the basement. *Why would she start there?*, Jean wonders. As if hearing her thoughts, Elena turns toward Jean. "You really must see this first. It's exquisite."

This lady better answer all my questions, Jean thinks as she follows Elena down the steps. Each one brings them closer to a clearly unfinished basement. The water heater, a blue cylinder about as big as the refrigerator upstairs, sits on the floor. A few feet away is a clunky furnace. A few old throw rugs are scattered about the concrete floor. Gray cinder blocks form the walls. The space is dark, damp and chilly. Jean wraps her arms around herself.

"Now this, this is what you've got to have a look at," Elena says, pointing toward a shelving unit lined with glass jars and cans of food that must have been down here for decades. Most of them are dented or rusty, with torn labels.

"Some old jars on a dusty shelf?" Jean balks. "How is that exquisite, as I believe you said?"'

Elena flashes a brilliant smile before she pulls a lever attached to the wall just above her shoulders. A suction noise startles Jean. It sounds like air is swooshing out of the room. She watches with fascination as the shelf gently shifts to the left, slowly and steadily as if it's on a track. A rush of warm air washes over Jean as the moving shelf reveals a hole in the wall. The sensation sends a ripple of goosebumps across her forearms. A soft hum emanates from its depths. The sound is relaxing, which is in complete contrast to how it looks – eerie and empty.

"Go ahead and take a closer look," Elena urges. "I'll turn some more lights on." Jean hears a faint click and a trail of dull glowing lights appear. Curiosity fuels her steps as she moves closer. She sticks her head through the opening. The dark gray walls are made of an intricately carved series of lines that rise and fall in a pattern. If she ran her fingers over them, they'd feel like ridges, rounded along their edges, but maze-like nubs that stick out of the walls. Small dots of light form random patterns along the floor and walls. There is no ceiling, only roundness, like a giant horizontal tube. The hum grows a little louder, as if it's encouraging her to enter. She glances at Elena, who nods encouragingly.

When she fully steps inside, it's like she's passed through a cloud that spit her out on the other side. Her body feels weightless as if she's floating in a sea of warm nothingness. She's vaguely aware of her senses – everything is muted. Her vision is blurred. All she can make out is the soft lights like distant stars in the sky. Her body seems to float in what feels like a silky bath that envelops her in peace. Each breath sets her more at ease, as if she's wrapped in a cozy blanket, soothed and calm.

Time doesn't seem to exist here. After what could be a few minutes or a few hours, the light shines brighter. She squeezes her eyes shut. Thoughts form in her brain, almost like voices – each one varying in tone and timbre. Some high-pitched, some deep, all ageless.

We're all around you, Jean. We look just like you and all the others you see walking down the street or passing by you at the grocery store.

"What?" she asks into the nothingness, confused yet content to hover in a state of oblivion.

This is our planet now. Every day hundreds of us replace hundreds of you.

Questions weave through Jean's mind, drifting into each other.

"What are you?" she thinks, grasping for cohesive thoughts.

We're like you, only stronger, faster and smarter. We're a superior species and the Earth has been damaged by humans for far too long. Think of us as missionaries of hope. We are the only ones who can restore nature and ensure that it is never treated as a commodity again. We've prospered on our own planet without destroying its beauty or its inhabitants. We can do the same here.

"H-how is this possible?" she wonders, not expecting an answer.

After millions of years, we finally found a way. And now that we have, there's no stopping us. But you've been chosen, Jean. You're going to help us.

"Help you?" The question flashes in her mind, although she can't form the words.

Yes, you see, this portal is just one entry point for our species, but it's not enough. We need more of them. Then, you will find others to join us.

She vaguely wonders what this means. Her own voice echoes in her mind, asking, "What will I do?"

We'll guide you. We're with you now. Just follow your thoughts and you'll be fine.

Time is meaningless in this comforting state. Completely relaxed, she absorbs every detail the voices share – how to find others like her, how to create a portal in her own home and how to recruit more humans to be hosts. When the lights fade, gentle hands wrap around Jean's arms, guiding her to walk forward. As awareness washes over her, Jean's gaze lands on Elena. She stares at the woman for a moment, confused, before recognizing the face on the open house sign.

"I'm so glad you came here today." Elena brushes her long dark hair behind her shoulder and rubs Jean's back before leading her to the front door and seeing her out.

Jean wanders along the sidewalk, trailing off to follow the footpath that snakes around her home. She slips inside the back door, closing it tightly before meandering to the kitchen sink. She dabs dishwashing liquid on a sponge and runs it under cold water, squeezing it out before gliding it along the green marble countertop.

"You finally back?" Hal calls from the living room. "You were over there a long time."

"I didn't realize how nice that house is inside," she answers. "I took a tour and it got me thinking."

"Thinking about what?" he asks, walking into the kitchen.

"Just that you should go see it too. It gave me some ideas about how we can fix the house up," Jean says dreamily before she turns to face him. "Go on over before the open house is over. Make sure you ask to see the basement."

SHROUDED VENUS

"It's not Christmas without a real tree!" Chase whines. "All my friends have real trees at home. I'm the only one with some stupid fake thing."

"I told you, I can either buy groceries and we put up the fake tree or we just go hungry but have a great-smelling live tree around for a few weeks." Janie's patience is wearing thin. She takes a deep breath and reminds herself that her son is only ten years old. He's not trying to be difficult. She softens her tone and continues. "Look, I can't afford it. If your father would just help with child support every now and then . . . "

She lets that last thought trail off. She and Tim agreed to keep their conflicts private, but this is all his fault. Maybe if he contributed anything, she wouldn't have to scrape by every month.

"I hate it here!" Chase huffs. He grabs his coat and backpack and storms out the front door.

Well, one less thing I have to do then. If he doesn't want our fake tree, I won't bother wrestling with it and trying to coax it to stand up straight, Janie thinks. She drops Chase off at school before continuing to the diner, where she tugs on an apron and readies herself for eight hours of chasing down people's orders, carting heavy loads of plates around and dealing with impatient customers.

By some stroke of luck, she's assigned to the counter this morning. It's all around easier, tending to couples or individuals all just a few feet away from you in any direction. It's just the breather she needs. When one of the regulars comes in, she grabs a mug and fills it to the rim with steaming black coffee. She sets it down in front of him just as he drops into his usual stool.

"Well, thank you, miss." Hank lifts the brown baseball cap from his head and sets it on the counter. Janie smiles, but he notices it looks forced. "What's wrong, little lady? And don't even try to deny it, because it's painted all over your face."

"Oh, my kid." She shrugs, rolling her eyes. "Said he hated living with me this morning."

"Now why's that?" Hank asks. "How could anyone hate living with you?"

She exhales a sigh and picks up a dishcloth, explaining as she wipes the counter. "It's stupid really. He wants a live Christmas tree but I'm not about to waste money on something that's going to drop needles all over my floor until I throw it out in a few weeks."

Hank pounds a fist on the counter, drawing a few stares. "Why I've got just the answer for you!"

Janie's narrowed eyes give away her disbelief. She crosses her arms and leans back against the counter behind her.

"No, really, I think I have the perfect solution," Hank says. He leans in closer, as if he's got a secret to share. "One of my buddies drives a garbage truck. Just yesterday, at poker night, he was telling us about one of his pickups."

Janie listens with interest even as she wonders, *What does this have to do with me and my kid's latest tantrum?*

"There's a lab on the outskirts of town. Every time my buddy makes a pickup there, it's weird stuff. And lately it's been piles of plants and trees."

Janie's eyebrows jump. Finally, something useful. "What kind of trees?" she asks, trying to temper the hope bubbling in her chest.

"Not exactly pine trees, some sort of hybrid stuff, but throw some tinsel on it and some of them twinkling lights, and you may be able to make it work. And the best part is, it would be free." Hank smiles and sits back in his chair, raising the mug to his mouth. After he takes a sip, he says, "You want me to ask my buddy if he could find you something? Hell, maybe he'd even drop it off at your house."

Tears prick the corners of her eyes as her hand flies to cover her mouth. "Oh Hank, that would be amazing. I can't thank you enough! Yes, if he can do it, I'll take whatever he can get. Chase and I can make it look festive! He'll be so excited!"

"Now there's that smile I like to see." Hank winks at her. "You write down your address for me. I'll call my buddy and see what he can do. With any luck, you'll have a tree set up tonight."

"Mom, a big truck just pulled up outside!" Chase yells from the living room.

"It's probably someone for the neighbors," Janie says, not bothering to look up from the stack of bills she's organizing by their due dates.

"A man just got out and he's walking up our sidewalk!"

Janie rises from the table and strides to the front door. Just as she pushes past Chase, three quick raps announce a visitor.

Janie gulps before cautiously opening the door. "Can I help you?" she asks, peering at the tall stranger dressed in a red flannel shirt and worn jeans.

"Hi, I'm a friend of Hank's and I have a delivery for you." He rocks back on his heels and glances at the house number. She lets out a small sigh of relief and her posture instantly relaxes.

"Oh, right, I forgot all about that. It's been a busy day." She presses a palm to her forehead. "Thank you so much! I really appreciate it. I appreciate you and Hank helping me out." Chase sneaks up behind her and peeks at the man.

"It's no problem, really." He points toward the truck with his thumb. "Okay if I bring it inside? It's just in the flatbed."

"Yes, please, can I do anything to help?" she asks eagerly.

"Just be ready to open the door," he calls as he turns toward the truck. With the man's attention focused elsewhere, Chase squeezes past Janie to get a better view.

"What's he talking about? What's he got for us?" Chase asks. She ruffles his hair, relieved she can finally do something to make him happy.

"You'll find out soon enough! It's a surprise!" With that answer, he squeals. She rests her hands on his shoulders as they watch the man lower the hitch and slide out what looks like a body wrapped in a blue tarp. It's nearly as tall as him, and he stands at least a foot over her thin five-foot five-inch frame. The man wraps his arms around the bundle and drags it toward the house.

This is a win. A small one, but still a win. It's their first Christmas since the divorce, and everything seems to be ten times harder than it was when she was still married – paying all the bills on her own, helping Chase with homework, planning meals. The list never ends.

Chase yanks her back to the present as he mutters under his breath, "Whatever it is, it's big."

"You sure you don't need a hand?" she calls before the man waves her off. As he nears, she guides Chase out of the way and swings the door wide open. "Could you put it right in the middle of the living room? Chase, show him where we want our Christmas tree."

The man sets the tree down with a thud and peels away the tarp. Janie's expression turns to confusion when he unwraps the blue vinyl, unveiling the large plant. Chase's mouth drops open as he stares. Janie can't help but ask, "What . . . what is that?"

"Well, it's not your . . . traditional . . . tree, but it's still a tree. There's this place just outside of town. They do all kinds of experiments and stuff. Weird stuff. Anyway, when they're done, they dispose of their . . . subjects. This was one of them. With a little love, I bet it'll be just fine." He folds the tarp and sets it on the floor before centering the tree in the space and taking a few steps back.

Its narrow trunk rests in a plastic black pot. Unlike the rough ridges bark usually forms, this looks like scales. The smooth, grayish plates line the trunk, disappearing beneath the branches. The branches are like long narrow fingers that stretch to the floor. Green and yellow leaves intermingle, crowding each drooping branch. They hang like a weeping willow. A gnarly, unhealthy one.

Janie gulps. It's hideous. This was a mistake. She should ask the man to take it away. Just as she opens her mouth to ask one more favor of him, Chase turns to her, buzzing with excitement. "This is awesome! We don't have to put up the fake tree! Can we decorate it now?"

Fighting every instinct, she smiles at her only child and nods. "You go get the ornaments. They're in the hallway closet."

As he tears off to retrieve the box of red and gold balls, she turns to the man. "This thing's kind of creepy-looking. Don't you think?"

He tilts his head, looking it up and down. "That little guy doesn't seem to mind. It might look pretty good after it's all done up, but there's only one way to find out."

"You're right, I'm being too critical," she admonishes herself. "Thank you, thank you so much for helping us. We really appreciate it."

"You're welcome, ma'am, and Merry Christmas." He tilts his head toward her and she leads him to the door.

"Merry Christmas to you too!" She watches him follow the walkway to his truck and locks the door after he starts to drive away.

She and Chase spend the next hour wrapping the tree in flashing multicolored lights and hanging balls on its branches until they run out. When Chase's stomach growls, reminding her that it's past dinnertime, they move to the kitchen to start their nightly routine.

Janie tosses noodles into a pot of boiling water as Chase empties his backpack on the kitchen table. In between setting the table and seasoning the sauce, she checks on his progress with completing a few worksheets and spelling lists. After they eat and clean up, it's already time for Chase to shower and hop into bed. When she tucks him in, he asks for an extra hug and kiss and thanks her for the tree.

With a bounce in her step, Janie pads down the stairs to the living room. She glances at the tree as her finger rests on the light switch. *Maybe it's not so bad,* she thinks. *It makes Chase happy, and it won't be around for that long. As soon as the holidays are over, we'll drag it to the curb with the trash, and we'll never have to see it again.*

She gasps when a branch rustles. She was staring right at it. There's no breeze and the heat vents are on the opposite side of the room. She inches toward the green and yellow monstrosity, watching it intently, ready to bolt if anything jumps out from the limbs. Her eyes catch no movement, and after a few minutes, she dismisses it as an overactive imagination. Her mind needs a break. She yawns, flips the light off and tiptoes to her bedroom so she doesn't wake Chase.

The next morning, Janie wakes with a smile on her face. Snippets of her dreams last night flash through her mind – a perfect Christmas morning, she and Chase wearing matching pajamas, him giggling as he tears into dozens of presents surrounding the tree. Of course, it's a dream. She has exactly four presents for her son, and it's the best she can do. But this is the start of their new lives, and each year will get better and better. Especially if she can track down Tim and file for child support.

Checking her clock, she's surprised to see it's 9:07 a.m. Chase never sleeps late, even on a Saturday. He should have bounded into her room two hours ago, demanding breakfast. She slips on a robe and rushes out the bedroom door as she ties the thin fabric belt around her waist.

"Chase, honey, good morning. Where are you?" She peeks into his small bedroom. Empty. His pillow is turned sideways and the blankets are a jumbled mess. She dashes downstairs, expecting to hear cartoon voices coming from the TV, but it's quiet. She tries again. "Chase! Where are you?"

Panic creeps into her mind as she runs from room to room, checking but not finding her son. She openly sobs, calling his name as she checks the front door. Still locked. So he didn't leave and no one came inside. Swiping away hot tears, she inhales a few deep breaths. *It's okay. He's probably just playing hide-and-seek. Calm down and check his hiding places,* she commands herself.

Janie sweeps back the shower curtain, peers beneath both of their beds and rummages through every closet in the small house. There's no sign of him anywhere. She slumps onto the couch and drops her head in her hands. After squeezing her eyes shut, trying to produce a logical explanation, she opens them. A small white tag hanging on the bottom of their new tree catches her attention. She didn't notice it last night.

She drops to her knees and crawls toward it. As she nears, she spots a few dark reddish-brown splatters on the floor. *Is this thing dropping some kind of sap,* she wonders. *Just great. My kid's missing and this hideous thing is ruining my carpet.* She runs her fingers over the spots. They aren't sticky, like sap would be. The dried substance forms rough little ridges in the carpet. Narrowing her eyes at the stupid tree, she notices the tag again and snatches it. The two words printed on it are no help: **Shrouded Venus**

"Is that what this thing is?" she asks no one. "What does that even mean?"

She crumples to the floor, unsure what to do next. In between her tears and sniffles, she hears a sound. Silencing herself, she prays it's Chase. She lies completely still, listening for anything that could be a clue. A subtle shifting, almost like slithering, whispers all around her. Movement flashes from above. Vines, thick as Janie's wrist, unfurl from the top of the tree.

They roll down, stopping with a snap. At the end of each one is an open mouth with two rows of narrow teeth as sharp as nails. In the blink of an eye, the vines wrap around Janie's arms and legs, holding her in place. She screams as the open jaws lower until they hover just inches from her face. Her last thoughts jump to the tag she pulled off the tree.

Of course. They called this thing a Shrouded Venus. A Venus flytrap, hidden, just waiting for an unsuspecting victim.

Fools Fest

"AND HOW ABOUT ONE more round of applause for Jake the Jokeman, our final performer at this year's Fools Fest!" The greasy-haired announcer lowers his microphone and raises his hands as if presenting the short, stocky comedian who waves before dashing behind the stage curtain. When the audience's cheers and clapping begin to fade, he raises the mic back to his mouth. "Thank you all for being here for this epic celebration of our thirteenth Fools Fest weekend. We couldn't have done it without you! Now, enjoy this last night together. Drink up, stuff your face and share some more laughs before we all head back to reality tomorrow." He tucks the mic back into its stand and circulates around the room, trading small talk with some of the more enthusiastic – louder, drunker – guests.

"You ready?" Katie asks, yawning and sliding her empty glass to the center of the rickety wooden table.

"One more?" Gus counters, raising his eyebrows in question as a devilish grin spreads across his cheeks.

She rolls her eyes but nods. "Fine, but make it fast. I'm tired."

Propping an elbow on the table, Katie rests her head against her open palm. When her gaze drops to the black-and-white checkered tile floor, her mind swims with dizziness as the busy pattern seems to shift with each passing second.

Gus raises his arm, motioning to a nearby waiter. Less than five minutes later, his frosty mug of golden liquid is delivered. Just like everyone else crammed at the square and circular tables surrounding the small stage, he lifts the glass to his lips and swallows a big swig.

Katie rubs her temples as the voices around them grow louder, fueled by liquor. She wonders if she's outgrowing their annual trip, surrounded by virtual strangers. Sure, there are some regulars who've been coming for years too, but they're just casual acquaintances – no one Katie or Gus associate with outside of this one gathering each year. When they first arrived Friday evening, the party atmosphere was a welcome reprieve from the monotonous workweek, but now it feels like everyone around her talks too loud, slurring their words in some unspoken competition to crack the best one-liner in between guzzling drink after drink.

As soon as Gus chugs the last drops of his beer, they head up to their room. Katie brushes her teeth, washes away the day's makeup and changes into her pajamas. When she finishes and slips out of the bathroom, Gus is already asleep in bed, complete with his shoes on. She chuckles to herself before untying his sneakers and slipping them off his feet. She doesn't bother waking him, figuring he just needs to sleep it off.

~ Two hours later ~

BEEEP! BEEEEEP! BEEEEEEEEP! BEEEP! BEEEEEP! BEEEEEEEEP!

The repetitive string of high-pitched tones yank Katie from sleep, launching her nerves into a thundering panic. Her senses hone in on the sound – her cell phone sits on the nightstand. Its screen flashes, a blinding beacon slicing through the dark room. Her hand scrambles toward it, fingers stumbling upon the device as its buzzing becomes incessant. She clutches it and raises it to her face, flinching as the brightness blurs her vision.

"What the—?" Gus grumbles. "Turn the damn phone off!" He scrunches a pillow over his head. She ignores him and focuses on the message. An exclamation mark, framed by an urgent red triangle, precedes the words. Black letters in all caps seem to shout EMERGENCY ANNOUNCEMENT.

She drags in a ragged breath as her mind struggles to comprehend what her eyes see.

This is a message from the emergency broadcast system. The United States is under attack. Several major cities have become targets of chemical warfare. These terrorist attacks are causing extreme health disorders within hours of exposure. If you are hearing this message, your area is within a target zone. Remain where you are – this is a shelter-in-place order. An antidote will be delivered to all commercial and residential businesses in your vicinity within eight hours. This shelter-in-place order remains in effect until all citizens within the target zone have received the antidote.

If you experience extreme symptoms of dizziness, fever, aches and confusion, call your local hospital or medical facility immediately. If you meet the criteria for immediate treatment, a police or military escort will direct you to the closest evaluation site. Stay tuned for more updates as they become available.

Katie presses a shaky hand over her gaping mouth, rereading the message. Worried it might disappear, she takes a screenshot before turning to Gus. He's completely oblivious, faintly snoring beneath the pillow. She shakes him.

"Wake up! This is serious." Still grasping the phone, she thrusts it toward him. When he merely grunts, she tears the pillow away and tosses it aside. He cracks an eyelid open but flinches from the glowing screen.

"What? What is it?" He massages his forehead and pinches his eyes closed.

"It's an emergency alert. It says that we're under attack. The country . . . the U.S. is under attack." Her shrill tone climbs higher with each word.

"An attack? Like aliens?" Gus busts out laughing, nearly falling off the bed. Katie stares at him as fear, frustration and anger collide within her.

"Did you hear me?" she asks, though it comes out more like a command than a question. She doesn't wait for him to answer. She shoves the phone in his face. "Read this!"

Rubbing his temple with one hand, he holds the phone with the other. She watches his eyes track left to right as he reads the message. When he finishes, he hands the phone back to her and scrunches his features in disbelief.

"So you know what today is, right?" he asks. When she purses her lips into a tight line and crosses her arms, he continues. "It's April Fool's Day. This has to be a joke!"

"You really believe that? How would the emergency alert send a message to everyone's phones?"

"Did you ever think maybe it's just everyone in this hotel right now? They probably have our cell phones on record. It's one last joke, the biggest joke, of the weekend."

Doubt weighs in the pit of her stomach as she turns over his words. They spent the last seventy-two hours gorging themselves on beer and greasy bar food while listening to a dozen different comedians. But that was something specific they paid for. This broadcast is going out to everyone. Right? Hot tears burn her eyes as she wonders if this is all some stupid trick. Maybe this really is a joke and no one outside of this place got that message.

"Babe, let's go back to sleep," Gus pleads. "We'll see if the message is still there in the morning. I bet it's just an epic prank though." He rolls over and buries his head in the pillow.

Blowing out a shaky breath, Katie presses a palm to her forehead. "I'm going downstairs and see if the front desk knows anything. If the hotel really did this, they've taken things too far."

"If it'll make you feel better," Gus mutters. "But don't wake me up when you find out it's all part of their master plan."

Smoothing her long dark hair down with her hands, Katie deems herself presentable enough, especially given what could be a national emergency. She quietly slips out the door, carefully pulling it closed. Padding to the elevator, she punches the down arrow. When the doors part to the lobby, she's met with quiet.

"Why isn't everyone down here?" she mutters to herself, scanning the small maze of couches and chairs across from the front desk. There are only four other guests in the lobby area – three women and one man. They form a small huddle, but their tentative proximity makes it obvious they don't know each other. Katie wonders if they came down here for the same reason she did.

As Katie wanders closer to the front desk, the employee standing behind it catches her eye. "Do you need help, miss?"

"I got . . . my phone went off. I got some emergency message." When the woman watches her, waiting, she continues. "Is it some kind of joke, like part of the Fools Fest experience?" Katie instantly regrets the question when the woman's eyes narrow on her.

"No, miss. That message was nothing that came from the hotel." The woman shakes her head slowly, punctuating her response.

"So it's not some sort of joke?" Katie's heartbeat spikes. The woman has already answered her question. There's nothing left to say, yet she remains planted in place, as if a better answer will come if she just asks it another way.

"We wish it were a joke, miss." The woman's features soften and her shoulders relax. The shiny gold name badge reads Christie.

"Okay." Unsure what else to say, Katie meanders to the small group of guests. As she draws nearer, she overhears their conversation.

"Is anyone gonna call their families? Like back home?"

"No, not in the middle of the night. What if they aren't in this quarantine zone, or whatever it is?"

"Could this really be legit?"

"Why aren't more people down here? Are we the only ones who think this is real?"

At that last question, Katie injects her thoughts. "Well, my husband's upstairs sleeping off a hangover. He thinks this whole thing is a joke. Maybe most of the people staying here are in various states of consciousness right now."

After about ten minutes of trading questions that no one has any answers to, the others return to their rooms, defeated. Katie slumps onto one of the soft chairs, contemplating what to do. No one seems to be taking this seriously. Does that mean everything's under control and the government or cops or whoever is taking care of it, whatever is happening, and by morning it will all be cleared up?

She relaxes into the cushions as her mind spins with endless questions. At some point, exhaustion drags her under its veil and she rests her head in the crook of her elbow, allowing her eyes to drift closed. Just as she starts to doze, the hotel doors swish open and the echo of fast-moving feet clacks across the tile floor, the sound bouncing off the walls. She yawns, jumping when a loud thunk startles her. Narrowing her eyes, she seeks the source of the abrupt noise, fully intending to share a look that conveys her annoyance. But when her gaze lands on the perpetrator, she rises with keen interest.

A man wearing a navy blue uniform stands at the front desk, speaking to Christie, the employee Katie talked to. Turning toward the glass windows, Katie notices an ambulance parked just outside the main entrance. The emergency lights flash but no sirens blare. He must be an EMT.

He points to a cardboard box on the counter and presents a paper to Christie, as if reviewing instructions. She listens intently and nods her head every few seconds. He hands her the paper, waves a hand in the air and dashes back out the entrance. Katie watches him hop into the ambulance, slam the door and drive away.

"Psssst."

Katie turns to find Christie motioning for her to come closer. As if in a trance, she wanders to the desk.

"I know you had questions, and I don't have much information," Christie leans closer, her voice just above a whisper, "but we got word that medication would be delivered sometime overnight. Ours just got here. It's iodine pills. We're supposed to give one to each guest and ask that they take it before they leave the premises."

Katie scrunches her face. "Iodine pills?" The emergency message didn't say that specifically, but it did mention an antidote.

"Supposedly they counteract, or I guess prevent, whatever this chemical agent is." The woman hunches her shoulder up in a shrug. "Anyway, I know you were really worried and we have to give them all out anyway, so if you want yours now, I can give it to you and just mark that your room already got them."

Katie nods feverishly. "Yes, please, thank you! I need two." She's the first one to get the antidote, all because she waited when everyone else gave up and went back to their rooms. A rush of pride sweeps through her.

With a conspiratorial smile, Katie accepts the small clear packets that each hold two thick, round white pills. With a renewed sense of urgency, she dashes to the elevator and zips up to the fourth floor. Slipping into the room, she goes directly to the bathroom and fills a glass with water. Swallowing her two pills, she refills the glass and sets it on the nightstand. She gently shakes Gus. When he doesn't move, she tugs on his arm impatiently.

When he finally responds, she asks him to sit up. He begrudgingly complies. After she explains what she saw and heard in the lobby, she hands him the medication and the glass.

"If I take these, you'll go to bed?" he asks. "And let me sleep?" She nods feverishly.

"Fine." He downs the chalky pills and hands the empty glass to her. She smiles, deposits it on the nightstand and climbs into bed beside him.

Now, she can finally relax.

~ Four hours later ~

Sunlight spills into the room, announcing the morning's arrival. Gus squints to ward away the unwelcome brightness. Just as he's about to wake Katie, both of their phones shriek. It's the same beeping pattern as last night. It must be an update.

Katie's eyes snap open as she's jolted from sleep. Her hand instinctively scrambles for her phone. Gus does the same. Before reading the message, they turn to each other. Stunned silent, their gazes run up and down each other.

Their once-brown irises glow a golden yellow. Squiggly red lines snake from their unusually large pupils to the cloudy edge of each eyeball. It makes them look feral, almost inhuman. Their faces are gaunt, overcome with a grayish pallor. Their fingernails, yellowed and cracked, are overgrown, jutting past the skin in sharp spikes.

What the hell did we drink last night, Gus wonders. When the repeating alarm beeps drag them from their momentary shock, they focus on the latest emergency message.

This is a message from the emergency broadcast system. We have a new development in the public emergency, and it is imperative that every person within the target zone follow these instructions carefully. If you were given an antidote for the chemical attack, do not consume the medication that was delivered. Repeating, do not take the medication that was delivered. While it was reported yesterday that the U.S. was under attack by chemical warfare, and antidotes were provided to hospitality businesses and residences over the past eight hours, we have new information indicating that the antidote was actually the weapon. The iodine pills trigger the extreme health disorders. If you have any medication in your possession, destroy it immediately. If you have already taken the medication, call 9-1-1 immediately.

Gus' jaw drops open. "What the hell did we do?" The couple shares a concerned glance before pounding erupts from the other side of their door. They scramble, tripping over their own feet as the frantic knocking continues. Before either one can twist the handle, a female voice calls, "Are you in there? It's Christie . . . from the front desk." Her tone is shrill, panicked, as if she's on the verge of hysteria.

When they yank the door open, Christie blurts out, "Those pills I gave you, I need them back!" She narrows her eyes as she takes in their disheveled appearance.

Katie and Gus turn to each other. A low growl rumbles from the back of Gus' throat as Katie's lips spread into a maniacal smile. Without another word, they both lunge at their visitor.

RejuvePet

Sarah's foot taps the floor as her eyes scan the waiting room. A TV is perched on the wall directly in front of her, blasting a game show originally recorded about thirty years ago. The feathered hairstyles and dated clothing are dead giveaways, not to mention the low-definition picture and the host's ridiculous jokes that would have been risque then but just sound idiotic in these vulgar modern times. The perfectly timed laugh track pushes her irritation to a new level.

Tuning out the show, Sarah scans the dull gray walls that seem to close in around her. They would be completely drab and depressing if not for the handful of framed portraits of doctors flashing brilliant white teeth, each one a perfect picture of happiness, hugging or holding their own beloved pet. Of course, they'll probably never know the raw anguish coursing through Sarah. They would all know exactly what to do if something was wrong with their animal. All she could do was gather Jack in her arms and drive him here as fast as traffic and the law would allow.

She laces her fingers together in a tangle of anxiety. They're slick with sweat. Unable to sit one second longer, she rises. Her legs are weak and her throat is dry. A faint pounding grows behind her eyes. The nerves jumbling within her will only feed the impending migraine. She pinches her eyes closed and rubs her temples. Frustration builds as she wonders how long she's supposed to sit here, just waiting, when her baby is back in some sterile room, all alone except for the vet and a technician or two.

If only Jack's leash hadn't slipped out of her hand, he would have never run out in front of that car. *Besides that, why was that idiot driving so fast,* she wonders. Everyone's in such a hurry these days. He was probably looking at his phone – distracted. Practically everyone is, and they don't care how it affects others.

In this case, the car's impact nearly killed Jack. After the initial horror and shock, Sarah pulled herself together enough to load Jack in her car and drive straight to the vet's office. They tried to send her to an emergency vet but her baby needed help and she refused to leave. After wasting precious minutes arguing, they finally agreed to help him, making sure to spell out that they could only do so much. Maybe instead of taking the time to declare defeat before even trying, they should have rushed him back to their fancy equipment to fix him.

Opening her eyes, she wanders around the waiting room, eager for any distraction that does not involve a game show. She spies a floor-to-ceiling bulletin board by the entrance and walks toward it. Her gaze slides over every paper pinned to it – an advertisement for overpriced flea treatment, announcement of an upcoming clinical study, local rescue group flyers, a poster of a missing dog and a picture of a cat someone is looking to rehome.

Then she sees it. One flyer is different than all the others. She takes a step closer to inspect it. The thick border is made up of picture blocks that line the whole outer edge. All the photos are people and their happy pets – families with teenagers, an older adult, a young couple. They are either cradling a cat or hugging a dog. Her eyes freeze when she notices the tan and black German Shepherd staring lovingly at a middle-aged couple. He looks just like Jack. Sarah's heart clenches. She presses a fist to her mouth and blinks fast, trying to contain the emotions threatening to spill out.

While the images initially draw Sarah's attention, the scripty text in the center of the page freezes her in place. Her eyes narrow and her jaw drops.

RejuvePet

Is your beloved pet at the end of their life? We can't reverse time, but we can delay it!

If you can't bear the thought of losing your most loyal companion, call us. RejuvePet's cutting-edge biomedical technology can extend your cherished family member's life.

It might not be time to say goodbye. Our professionals have helped hundreds of grateful pet owners. You could be next.

In smaller print, at the bottom of the page, it reads:

Best results if our procedure is done within two hours of your pet's passing.

Sarah takes a step back, as if putting distance between herself and the flyer could suddenly make it disappear. *Sick,* she thinks. *That's just sick. Who would believe that? Or ever try it? That can't be real.*

"Miss Roberts?" The receptionist's voice yanks Sarah's attention from the bulletin board.

"Yes?"

"Dr. Harkins is out of surgery. I can take you back to talk with her."

"Can't I see Jack first?" Sarah asks, rushing toward the woman. "Or just take me to him. She can talk to me there."

Pity creeps into the woman's gaze. She chews her bottom lip before answering. "It's best if you talk to Dr. Harkins first." Without another word, the woman turns and walks down the hallway. Sarah follows her eagerly. With a promise that the doctor will be right in, the woman slips out the door, leaving Sarah, consumed with anticipation, in the small examination room.

Less than five minutes later, Dr. Harkins sweeps into the room. Sarah's heart pounds as she shoots to her feet. The doctor's face says it all. She steps toward Sarah, placing a gentle hand on her trembling arm. "I'm so sorry, Miss Roberts. Jack didn't make it."

"Whaaaaaaa—" The word dies on Sarah's lips. Her chest constricts and she gasps for air. The room seems to close in on her. Everything feels wrong – the lights are too bright, Dr. Harkins is standing too close and suddenly her whole body feels too heavy, as if she can't support it.

Dr. Harkins helps her to a seat, offers her a box of tissues and leads her through some basic deep breathing exercises. After she's calmed down enough to listen, the doctor explains that Jack's internal injuries were much worse than they suspected. Although they tried every option available, there was nothing they could do to save him.

Sarah sobs openly as shock and pain war within her, rendering her mind nearly useless. When Dr. Harkins asks if she has any questions, Sarah just shakes her head slowly. She finds her voice when Dr. Harkins asks if she'd like the animal hospital to take care of a burial or cremation.

"No," Sarah cries. "Jack's coming home with me." She knows she should thank the doctor for everything they've done, but she can't in this moment. Every nerve ending feels raw. Weakness invades every cell of her body all the way to her limbs. It takes effort just to breathe.

Dr. Harkins escorts Sarah to the front desk while they prepare Jack's body for the ride home. As Sarah stands there, trying to stifle her sobs, her eyes wander to the bulletin board. She rushes over and snatches the RejuvePet flyer. Thrusting it toward the receptionist, she asks, "Is this real?"

The woman rolls her eyes and shakes her head. "Someone keeps hanging those flyers in our waiting room and we keep taking them down. We don't endorse that. It's clearly a scam preying on people in a compromised emotional state to believe something like that. I can take it and tear it up. We wouldn't want any of our clients to actually call that place."

"I'll throw it out for you," Sarah says, shoving the paper into her purse.

"You sure?" the receptionist asks skeptically.

As Sarah nods, a somber-faced technician walks through the office carrying a cardboard box. "Miss Roberts, I can follow you out to your car."

Sarah gulps and sucks in a ragged breath. What she wouldn't give to return to any of those moments where she and Jack walked through these doors together. Now he's leaving in a box. Reality stabs at her heart. He was her everything. She never married, never wanted kids. Jack was the only companion she ever needed. And now he's left her alone with her misery.

She forces her feet to move toward the blue Jetta haphazardly parked in the loading zone. She was in a such a hurry when they arrived, she didn't even notice where she left the car. Tapping the button to unlock it, Sarah opens the door to the backseat. The technician gently places the box on the cushion and offers some hollow consolation. *They're just words,* Sarah thinks. *They won't bring back my Jack.*

Avoiding the rearview mirror and any visual reminder of her only passenger, Sarah relies on muscle memory to lead the way home. She slows and stops when necessary, seeing but not feeling or truly absorbing the outside world. When she reaches the small Cape Cod house, she pulls into the driveway. After switching the car off, she glances at the backseat before resting her head on the steering wheel. Hot tears spill down her cheeks as she openly sobs. *This wasn't supposed to happen,* an agonized voice screams in her head.

Sniffling, she swipes away the mucus running from her nose. She grabs her purse and reaches inside, fumbling for a tissue. Instead, her fingers grasp paper. It's the crumpled flyer from the vet's office – for RejuvePet. She re-reads the ridiculous claims. Turning to the box on the backseat, she stares at the box. *What if there is something more I could do? What if I could get him back?*

With a shaking hand, she raises her phone. She dials the number and hangs up. "This is stupid," she chastises herself. "No one can do this, or I would have heard of it before." She sets the phone down. *But you have to at least try,* her mind whispers. *You'd never forgive yourself if you didn't do absolutely everything possible.* With a renewed resolve, she taps the numbers on the keypad, chewing her bottom lip as it rings.

"Hello," a deep voice answers.

"Um, yes . . . is this RejuvePet?" Sarah presses a palm to her forehead. *Stupid question,* she thinks, *but she wouldn't have to confirm if they had answered the phone with a professional greeting.*

"Yes, it is. Are you in need of our services?" His tone is even, calm. As if they aren't dealing with a life-or-death situation.

"Yes . . . I mean, I think so . . . but how are you even able to . . . you know." Tears well in her eyes as she clings to the last shred of hope holding her heart together.

"That's nothing for you to worry about," the man says, then more gently he asks, "How long ago did your pet pass?"

The mere question reignites the pounding behind her temples. A fresh wave of tears burns hot, preparing to spill. "Um, about . . . about an hour ago. But can you really do this? I can't take believing that you can save him and then losing him again."

"I can't promise anything, but I can try. Right now, time is the most important factor. The sooner you can get here, the better our chances of saving him are. Here's what you need to do."

The man can't see, but she nods as he rattles off instructions – write down the address, bring $5,000 in cash, get the body there as quickly as possible. She agrees, sets the phone down and drives to the bank. Sarah rushes to the first teller she sees – a short, pudgy woman whose eyes never stray from the keyboard as she processes the withdrawal request.

As the woman taps a few buttons, Sarah inhales a deep breath and rakes her fingers through her wavy dark hair. She must look awful. Her eyes feel puffy, swollen from all the tears she's shed today. She chews her bottom lip as she waits. The man at RejuvePet said to get Jack's body there as quickly as possible. She can't afford to waste time. Just as she's about to ask the teller how long this will take, the woman slides a drawer open and starts counting the money. With an envelope full of cash in hand, Sarah rushes out the door.

Once again, Sarah finds herself pacing but this time in a small, dated living room. Waiting reminds her of the vet's office. That didn't end well. She prays this time is better. She studies the room's contents to keep her mind busy. The moss green sofa is draped with a brown and orange crocheted quilt that looks like it's from the 1970s. Two plump pillows in the same yarn colors and pattern sit on the matching loveseat. She plops down on the sofa, releasing a small cloud of dust in the process. Dropping her head into her hands, she starts to tremble. *This is just delaying the inevitable. If this guy could really do what he says he can, he'd be rich. He wouldn't live in a home that clearly hasn't been updated in decades.*

After what feels like hours, the man emerges. Even before he swipes away his surgical mask, his broad smile is obvious. It reaches his eyes. Hope blooms in her chest.

"Is he, is he okay?" she dares to ask.

"We got him back!" The man's excitement is palpable. Sarah nearly collapses but the man reaches out and steadies her.

"Can I see him?" she asks as eagerness overtakes her.

"Of course. I'll wheel him out here on a gurney and help load him into your car. He hasn't woken up yet from the anesthesia, but he can go home."

"Oh thank you, I can't thank you enough."

"There's just one thing," the man says, seriousness replacing the happiness in his features. "The agreement you signed included instructions for his care. You must follow them exactly. You cannot deviate from them. At all."

"Sure, anything, I'm just glad to have my boy back." Sarah laughs. When the man wheels Jack out to the living room, Sarah's eyes zero in on his chest. It rises and falls methodically. *He's breathing.* Comfort washes over her. This was the best decision she's ever made. They walk outside to her car. As the man gently places Jack in the backseat, he hands Sarah some papers.

"Go home and let Jack sleep it off. While he's resting, read through my instructions so you're ready to feed him when he wakes up. He'll be hungry and needs to replenish his energy. Today really took a lot out of him."

Sarah nods and takes the paperwork. Driving home, she sings along with the radio, belting out whatever song comes on. When they arrive back home, she taps into the adrenaline from the day's turn of events and carries Jack inside. She places him in her bed and tiptoes out to the living room so that he can rest peacefully.

She kicks off her shoes and curls up on the couch, letting exhaustion sink in as her excitement wears off. After a few minutes of relaxing and clearing her mind, she remembers the agreement she signed. With a sigh, she rises and retrieves the paperwork. First on the list is to leave a review online. *Why didn't she think to check reviews of RejuvePet before she took Jack there?* It doesn't much matter, because they have an average of 4.8 from more than a hundred ratings and reviews. She adds her own, giving them 5 stars and a few sentences expressing her gratitude. With that done, she reads the next item on the list.

Buy food for your pet. This must be a living creature. Chicken, rabbit or squirrel is suggested for dogs, but any small mammal would suffice. Sarah barks out a laugh. Surely this must be a joke. She continues to read the paperwork but there is no asterisk or any other indication that this point is negotiable.

Sarah's stomach sours at the thought. *I'm not sacrificing some other animal for Jack,* she decides. *He's eaten the kibble I've fed him all his life. He doesn't even care about hunting. And how on earth would I get a rabbit?*

She glances to Jack's food and water bowls, sitting on the kitchen floor, waiting for him like they always are. She walks over, changes the water and replenishes the crunchy food. These have worked just fine for years and she's not changing it now, she decides. She checks on Jack one more time before readying for bed. It's not even nine o'clock but she's exhausted. Plenty of rest will do them both good.

A low snarl nudges Sarah from her sleep. Her eyes slide to the illuminated digital clock. 3:21 a.m. Jack stands on his hind legs, his paws resting on the bed. He growls.

"Hey, boy, what is it?" She reaches to pet his head but hesitates when their eyes lock. Even in the darkness, she can see that his are devoid of recognition or emotion. She leans away, putting a little distance between her and the dog. He lowers his head, hackles raised, and snarls again. This time with a fury she's never heard from him.

Before she knows what's happening, he lunges and jumps on top of her. She squirms, screaming, "Down! Get down, Jack!" Her command goes unheard. Before Sarah can react, he clamps his mouth around her throat.

"Ja—" His jaws constrict tighter, extinguishing her plea. Her eyes meet his as tears stream down her face, mingling with blood. His pupils are wide and his movements are eager. She tries to push him away, but he's so strong. Searing pain scorches her neck. She tries to wrap her hands around it, but they slip away, slick with warmth. Random thoughts flicker through her mind but she can't fully grasp any of them.

Jack shakes his head back and forth, ripping her flesh raw. Pain and terror collide within her. Her mind and body go numb. Her arms are too heavy to lift. She tries to speak, to tell Jack to stop, but can only manage an unintelligible gurgle. The dog greedily slurps muscle and nerves.

He's no longer a beloved pet. He's a predator. And she's his prey – his dinner.

THE LOYALTY CURE

"WHY ARE YOU DRIVING so fast?" Alyssa demands, wrapping her fingers around the door handle. "You've only told me about a zillion times to drive carefully, and here you are doing at least twenty miles over the speed limit. On super windy roads!"

"I'm just really excited for our mother-daughter day, that's all." Robin slows down slightly and grips the steering wheel tighter, focusing on the twists and turns ahead. It's the perfect excuse to avoid eye contact with her only child.

"Where are we even going? This looks like the way to Grandpap's cabin, not any sort of mall." Alyssa crosses her arms as her tone turns accusatory.

"Okay, you caught me," Robin chuckles, but it's clearly forced. "I needed to talk to you about something and I wanted to make sure we had complete privacy, so I thought we could spend the day at Pappy's cabin."

"What?" Alyssa shakes her head as annoyance flares. "You could have just told me we were going there. I was all ready for a day of clothes and shoes and purses. At least I could have mentally prepared for mud and humidity and bugs instead." She rolls her eyes before turning to the window, suddenly wishing she was anywhere but here.

"I didn't think you'd come if I told you the truth," Robin admits. "Besides, I didn't want you to tell anyone we were coming here."

"Oh my gosh. What is going on? Why are you acting like there's some super secret that we can't just talk about at home?" Alyssa's frustration soars with every passing minute.

"We'll talk when we get there. Just trust me, okay?"

An hour later, the sky-blue Honda Accord turns down the dusty, rocky path that barely constitutes a road. Pebbles pelt the undercarriage in their effort to chip away the paint one little ding at a time. When the car finally rolls to a stop, Alyssa throws the door open and jumps out. Her mood has simmered to mild disappointment.

"Sorry I got upset. I just wish I knew we were spending the day here. Maybe I would have worn boots or old sneakers." Alyssa shrugs.

"I understand," Robin says. "Let's just make the best of a beautiful day, okay?"

When Alyssa offers a small smile and nods, Robin pops the trunk open and motions for Alyssa to help her unload it.

"What is all this?" Alyssa asks as her eyes rove over the contents – a large blue cooler, a brown paper bag stuffed with snacks and a cloth grocery bag with a glass pitcher, paper plates and napkins, and plastic utensils. Loading their arms and shoulders, they empty the trunk and climb the rickety cabin steps. They drop everything on the narrow kitchen counter.

"Why don't you go sweep and I'll meet you out there in a few minutes?" Robin suggests. "I can mix up some drinks and get us some snacks."

"Okay." Alyssa turns on her heel and heads to the huge wraparound porch. When she was little, she loved coming to the cabin. The porch was her favorite part. It served as headquarters for her nightly firefly hunts. And sometimes, if they sat there and were really, really quiet, they'd see wildlife wander right up to it. She'd watch with awe as a mama bear would pass by with playful cubs trailing behind her. The deer were such frequent visitors that she lost interest in them, but seeing a fox or a raccoon always captivated her. She'd watch with fascination, or at least until a squeal escaped her and scared away whatever visitor happened to wander nearby.

Now, her growing distaste for biting insects, eerie nighttime sounds and the rustic accommodations outweighs her childhood memories. She sighs, certain her mother knew this trip wouldn't be well received. Otherwise, she wouldn't have lied about their destination.

After sweeping away every last cobweb and speck of dirt the broom can reach, Alyssa drops into an Adirondack chair. Robin appears a few minutes later, sets a tray down on the small table between their seats, and plops into her own chair. With glasses of sangria, brimming with a medley of fresh berries, and small plates of cheese cubes, crackers and almonds, they both sit back and enjoy the impromptu picnic.

When they finish, Alyssa rests her head against the seat back. "This was a really good idea, actually! I'm glad we did this."

Robin's smile quickly fades. "Could you do something for me?"

"Of course. What is it?" Alyssa asks, worry slices through her.

"Could you run our phones out to the car? Just lock them in there?"

Alyssa's eyes narrow and her nose crinkles. She waits for a punchline that doesn't come. Apparently, Robin's request isn't a joke.

"I just want to speak privately and I'd feel better if our phones weren't anywhere near us."

"Ooooookay." Alyssa stands. After Robin hands over her phone, Alyssa dashes inside the cabin to grab the car keys. She returns a few minutes later, breathing heavy from the exertion of rushing after downing a few glasses of alcohol.

"Okay, the phones are locked away. Now what is so top secret that you wouldn't tell me until now?" She drops into her seat and focuses every ounce of attention on her mother.

"It's work." Robin folds her hands and watches Alyssa's reaction.

"I thought everything was great? You just got that big promotion. So now instead of just being a regular epidemiologist, you're some kind of super epidemiologist." Alyssa smirks.

Robin chuckles but her features stiffen in seriousness too soon. Now, instead of just studying infectious disease patterns, causes and effects, her new role involves planning for outbreaks and pandemics. As she's been granted access to sensitive information and invited to attend meetings with national health experts, she's learned some dark secrets that don't seem to alarm anyone else involved.

According to internal, classified reports, most infectious diseases were eradicated in the U.S. decades ago. Now the government uses them to cull the population and eliminate threats. Where cures could be distributed, they are calculatedly withheld. Especially in high crime areas.

"If we continue on the path this economy is on, our homeless population will skyrocket," Robin explains. "We can't control it now, let alone if it increases. It's all a cycle – people lose their jobs, turn to crime, face homelessness. And instead of providing social support, our leaders would rather just rid themselves of the problem before it completely blows up in their face."

"That . . . that doesn't make sense," Alyssa stutters. "Doctors and hospitals all across the country are just going to let people die because we need to reduce the population? That would be all over the news."

"It's not, because they don't know about this. Some medications are placebos." Robin raises an eyebrow, waiting for Alyssa to recognize the connection. When she narrows her eyes in confusion, Robin continues. "The drug companies are given specific directions on when and where to provide full-strength medications or treatments and when not to."

Alyssa rubs her temples and squeezes her eyes shut. "This is a lot to take in. How could you know this?"

"It's been going on for years. I found reports and even copies of memos sent that detail placebo distribution. And it happens to correlate with the unhealthiest states in the country. West Virginia, Mississippi, Kentucky, Arkansas. That isn't just a coincidence. Those people are specifically targeted to decrease a growing population problem."

"What are you going to do?" It's the one question Alyssa can form as thoughts churn in her mind.

"I'll gather as much as I can on Monday morning and take it to the police. They'll need to get the FBI involved or some other national agency, but I don't know who I can trust at work, so I'm not even talking to anyone there about it."

"Do you think it's safe?" Alyssa asks, shivering from a sudden chill in the air.

"I'm going in very early in the morning. The only one there at that time is a security guard and they all recognize me. They know I have clearance to be there. I'll be in and out before anyone even notices." A sly smile plays across Robin's face. She's not taking any chances. Alyssa nods, hoping this will all be over soon.

When the sun nearly completes its daily trek toward the horizon, they clean up and lock the cabin. The drive back home is quiet. Before hopping in her car to head to her apartment, Alyssa wraps her arms around Robin, sharing a strong hug.

"I'm really proud of you, Mom. You're really brave."

"Oh, not brave. Just doing what's right." Robin waves off the compliment and wishes her daughter a safe drive.

8 a.m. Monday morning

"Hello?" Alyssa normally doesn't answer her phone when an unrecognized number flashes on the screen. But this time the caller ID shows it coming from a local hospital. She raises a trembling hand to cover her mouth as she listens to the calm but urgent voice on the other end.

"I'll be there as soon as I can," she says, running out the door before disconnecting the call. Just yesterday, she chastised her mother for driving too fast but today she weaves between vehicles, pushing the speed limit, earning a few beeping horns and one-fingered salutes. All she cares about is getting to the hospital. Flying into the closest parking spot she can find, she throws the car in park and rushes to the main entrance and the information desk.

"My mother was admitted a few hours ago. They said she had a stroke. I need to see her." The older man sitting behind the desk eyes her sympathetically.

"Sure, just give me her name and I can look her up for you."

Five minutes later, with a proper visitor's badge, directions and a destination, Alyssa takes off for the elevators. When she reaches the eighth-floor nurses' station, she announces that she needs to see her mother. A short, bald man in scrubs sidesteps around the desk and approaches her.

"I can take you to her room. She'll be glad to see you."

"Thank you."

"But before we go, you should know her limitations. She had a stroke and it appears to have caused some brain damage. We believe she has early signs of aphasia. It's a condition that prevents her from speaking and fully understanding language."

"You're telling me she has brain damage? And she can't communicate?" Alyssa's stomach churns with a blend of anticipation and fear of seeing her mother.

"We're still running tests on her, this is just our initial diagnosis. It's not conclusive. I just want you to be prepared in case she doesn't seem like herself."

Alyssa's pulse rockets when they reach the room. The nurse opens the door, closing it behind Alyssa when she crosses the threshold. When her eyes land on Robin, she pauses. Her heart stutters. The woman lying in bed looks like her mother, but a pale, weak version. Alyssa rushes to her side.

"Mom! What happened? I just saw you yesterday and you were fine!" Alyssa's eyes search for a hint of recognition in her mother's eyes. Robin raises an arm to greet her daughter and pulls her closer. Alyssa sits on the side of the bed and holds her mother's hands.

"Are you okay?" Alyssa demands. Robin shakes her head no. "Right, they told me you can't talk. But you can understand me, right?"

Robin shakes her head again but her eyes flutter and she dry heaves, as if the movement makes her nauseous.

"It's okay," Alyssa whispers, rubbing her mother's arm. "No more nodding. How about you blink fast for yes and squeeze my hand for no." Her voice breaks and she swallows the emotion forming a lump in her throat.

Robin's eyes flutter open and closed several times.

"This happened, you're here, because of what you told me yesterday." It's a question, but comes out as a statement.

Robin blinks.

"I don't know what to do." Any strength Alyssa felt fades and her posture drops like a rag doll. A coincidence she could handle. But now it feels like it's her against the world, and her mother is a pawn whose fate is her responsibility.

"Okay." She steadies herself, inhaling a deep breath. "You said you have evidence. If I can—" Before she can finish, Robin squeezes her hand, with much more strength than expected.

"What do you mean, no?" Alyssa asks sharply. "I have to do something!" Another quick squeeze of her hand.

"Why? Why would we just let this go? You have proof!" Robin squeezes again. Her eyes pool with tears. Alyssa gulps.

"If I try, they'll do something to me. Is that it?" Robin blinks so fast that Alyssa wonders if she's having some sort of seizure.

"You want me to let this go? Do nothing?" Hot anger burns in Alyssa's chest, bearing the weight of injustice and grief. It spreads through her like wildfire.

Robin squeezes her hand, this time unwilling to release her grip. She tugs three times.

"What? There's something else."

Robin motions with her hand as if she's writing.

"Paper! You can write a message!" Alyssa scours the room, searching for a tablet. This isn't a hotel. There's no little pen and paper sitting by the phone. She pushes through the door and runs to the nurses' station.

"Can I have a piece of paper and a pen?" The question sounds more like a demand, but she doesn't care. Excitement courses through her. A young nurse, probably only a few years older than Alyssa, grabs a sheet of blank paper from the printer and hands it over, along with a pen bearing the hospital's logo. Throwing a quick "thanks" and a wave over her shoulder, Alyssa dashes back to her mother's room. She wheels a tray over to the bed and plops the pen and paper on it.

She paces impatiently as Robin scribbles a note. It takes her several minutes. When she finally finishes writing, she sets the pen down and reclines back against her pillows. Alyssa takes the paper in her hands.

If I keep quiet about what I discovered, they promised me the loyalty cure. It will reverse the effects of the stroke, which they medically induced when they discovered my plan. It's a simple deal – either I shut my mouth or they'll shut it for me.

Alyssa backs into the wall and slides down, landing on her bottom. She just wants her mom back, healthy. The cost is too great, but they're unable to stop any of it from happening anyway. As a tear slides down her cheek, she nods at Robin once.

There's no choice but to accept the deal they've been offered.

Life Membership

As Landon breezes through the glass doors, his gaze shifts from one familiar sight to the next – parallel rows of treadmills, a cluster of stationary bikes and a grouping of elliptical machines. A tall man with mocha colored skin and close-cropped hair greets him from behind the front desk.

"I see you sporting that Infinity Fit t-shirt," the man says jokingly. "So either you're a super fan of the club or you're our newest employee." A smile glints in the man's dark eyes.

"Ha, yeah, I'm Landon, today's my first day, kind of." Landon approaches and thrusts an open hand toward the employee.

"Nice to meet you, Landon," the man says, wrapping his hand in a firm grip and shaking it. "I'm Carter. What do you mean today's *kind of* your first day here?" Carter quirks an eyebrow up as he waits for an answer.

"Well, my parents own the gym. I just got back from college. I'll be here all summer and they think I should make myself useful, I guess." Landon shrugs.

"Oh man, glad you told me that before I said anything bad about them." Carter holds a serious look for a few seconds before cracking up. "Just kidding, your parents are great. I've only been working here for a few months, but I really like it. Don't get me fired, okay?" Carter's cheeks flush crimson with the realization that he may have said too much.

"Nah, totally fine. Half the time I can't stand them." Landon chuckles, instantly deciding that he and Carter will get along great.

"Ah, I see you two have met." Landon's mom, Steph, steps out of her office. "We've made a few changes since winter break, so Carter, could you bring Landon up to speed on the new software program?"

"I'd be happy to." Carter flashes a wide grin. In between greeting members and blending smoothie orders, he shows Landon common commands and functions used during a typical shift. They're interrupted several times by members asking questions or people coming into the club to learn about equipment, classes and membership plans.

Time passes quickly. They fill each bit of free time by bantering about their favorite sports teams and trading jokes. By six o'clock, Landon's back and feet ache from standing all day.

"My shift's almost over, man. Do you know how to do the water additive?" Carter asks.

"The what?" Landon counters, narrowing his eyes.

"The additive." Carter pauses, as if that answer may trigger a memory. When Landon just scrunches his face in confusion, Carter adds, "They've been using it since before I started here. I just figured you'd know about it."

"No." Landon shakes his head. "I never heard of it and I work here every summer and break."

"All right, then let me show you." Carter motions for Landon to follow him to the storage room behind the front desk. The large closet area is crammed with boxes and cartons of protein powders, fruit purees, and disposable plastic cups and lids.

"This stuff," Carter says, pointing to the bright orange box labeled Immortazyne. A middle-aged man flexes his biceps on the label. "We drop two tablets in the water supply each day. Before you do it, check the clipboard." Carter motions toward a chart hanging on the wall just inside the door. "Make sure no one did it yet for the day. As long as they didn't, go ahead and do it and then sign your initials beside the date."

"What is this stuff? Like a fluoride or something?" Landon asks, picking up the box and turning it over to read the ingredient list. It's a string of chemicals, each one with a longer name. The description claims that the product enhances the body's natural functions like boosting the immune system, repairing and replacing unhealthy cells, and increasing the brain's neurotransmitter levels to improve mood. "Whoa, this is way more than fluoride," he mutters to himself.

"I don't really know, I just do what I'm told." Carter chuckles, raising his hands in the air as if proclaiming his innocence. "Anyway, in case you ever need to do it, you just drop them in this tank. It's the water softener. Open the lid and toss them inside. Once a day, every day. Your parents get pretty upset if someone forgets."

That doesn't sound right, Landon thinks but keeps it to himself. His parents are particular, they like things done a certain way, but it's not like them to get angry over something so minor. He shrugs it off.

They walk out of the storage area together so Carter can clock out for the day. Landon busies himself at the front desk, answering members' questions, ringing up any snacks or smoothies they purchase, and offering class schedules to anyone who asks about group fitness options.

When the evening rush empties out, Steph sweeps out of her office and joins Landon behind the desk. "You must be worn out. You're not used to working all day. It's almost closing time anyway, you want to head out? Dad and I can close up and meet you back at the house."

"If you don't need me," he answers, glancing at his watch.

"Nah, you did enough today," she says, smiling.

Landon reaches beneath the counter and grabs his car keys before clocking out. Just as he circles the counter, he turns toward his mother. "Hey, I meant to ask you, what's this water additive thing? Carter showed me how to do it. He said we've been using it since he started at least, but this is the first time I ever heard about it."

Steph's eyes widen with momentary surprise. She pinches her lips closed for a moment before responding. "Oh, don't worry about that. It acts like a filter, you know, to purify the water. I mean, it's pretty important to have palatable water at a gym."

"But—" he starts before she cuts him off.

"You're already clocked out, go on home. We'll catch up with you for dinner." She waves her hands dismissively, shooing him toward the exit.

"Okay," he calls behind his shoulder as he pushes through the door.

The house is quiet when Landon gets home. He crashes on his bed, giving his aching muscles a chance to relax. While he gets a lot of steps at school, walking to classes, he's also used to sitting for long periods of time, whether he's listening to a lecture or studying for exams. The job at the gym isn't hard, but it requires him to be on his feet all day.

As his body sinks into the mattress, he scrolls on his phone. When he tires of the mindless activity, his thoughts drift back to the additive Carter showed him – Immortazyne. *Why did his mom act weird about it?* He searches and scrolls, this time with a purpose. His adrenaline surges as he finds website after website of warnings and reviews for the product.

Several claim it's an addictive drug that changes the body's chemistry, acting like a preservative to prolong life. Every page makes more fantastical claims or criticisms than the last. *How can this be true?* A fast twenty minutes later, Landon's yanked from his intense focus by plates and pots clanking in the kitchen. He didn't even realize his parents were home. He was too caught up in his research.

Soon after that, Steph calls out, "Dinner's ready." Landon rushes down the steps, eager for a home-cooked meal. The dining hall at school was fine, but it doesn't compare to his parents' cooking. When they sit and pass around the serving bowls, he loads every square inch of his plate with tender roast beef, creamy mashed potatoes, thick gravy and plump green peas.

"So, was it good to be back at the club?" Steph asks as she stabs a forkful of meat.

"Yeah, I like that Carter guy," Landon says between bites. "But he showed me something I thought was kind of weird."

His parents glance at each other and wait in silence for him to elaborate.

"I know you said it was just to purify the water, but I did some research on that Immortazyne." He raises his eyebrows, waiting for them to ask what he found. When neither one does, he continues. "It sounds like that stuff is really bad. There are all kinds of articles about how it causes people to be addicted to it and it's like a preservative for their organs." He wrinkles his nose in disgust.

"Son," Frank says, "since we started using Immortazyne, business has skyrocketed. You saw how busy it was today. People really like the way it makes them feel. It's a win for everyone. We're giving them exactly what they want. It makes members want to come back, and frankly, the group fitness classes are overflowing and members often have to wait for their turn on a machine."

"We're at the point where we have to expand," Steph adds. "Open another location, and we'll need someone to manage it."

Landon's parents watch him with raised eyebrows and goofy grins.

"Wait, I would be in charge of a gym?" Landon asks, losing his resolve as he considers their offer.

"Who better to run it than you?" Steph says. "Someday it will all be yours anyway. You might as well have a hand in building it."

"With any luck, we'll have it ready to open by the time you graduate and you can step right into that role," Frank adds.

"Can't you do this without drugging people though? It feels . . . wrong." His stomach twists in knots, driving away any lingering hunger.

"Well, you didn't seem to have a problem with it when we paid your tuition bill each semester." Frank's tone sharpens. "Or rent for that fancy off-campus apartment."

"But I didn't know that's how you were getting the money." Landon runs a hand through his hair, leaving sandy-colored tufts sticking out in various directions.

'Well, now you know. Does it really change anything though?" Steph demands. "Our members come to improve their health, to feel better, to live longer. That's exactly what we're giving them. Hell, we should probably be charging them more for what they get."

"Look, you just got back, son. You worked one shift," Frank says, softening his tone. "Give it a chance. See for yourself how happy our members are. They feel great, they're building muscle and they're prioritizing their health. We found a winning formula. All we have to do is stick with it to be successful."

The dinner conversation shifts to small talk about the weather. As soon as he finishes eating, Landon excuses himself and retreats to his bedroom. He always figured he'll inherit the family business, but he never expected it to grow so fast. He has one more semester of college left, but if his parents' plans fall into place, he'd graduate with a job lined up and the freedom to build the business as he wants.

He showers and lies in bed, propping his laptop on his chest. What starts as watching random YouTube videos about dietary supplements quickly leads to people's accounts of using Immortazyne. Curiosity leads him to click and sit back while the next one plays. The videos range from people of all ages who improved their performance when they took the supplement to health experts and scientists who claim the chemicals in it cause hardened arteries, weaker bones and thinner blood. They also warn that it can cause drug interactions for people who take multiple medications, and some reactions can be fatal.

Hours later Landon's head pounds and his vision blurs. He closes the laptop and readies for sleep. He's learned enough about this product. He just needs to find a way to keep his parents happy and clear his conscience.

The next morning, Landon arrives at the gym excited to start the day. He talks to his coworker, a middle-aged woman, the minimal amount possible to still be considered friendly. Feigning interest in the new computer program, he asks if she can handle any members' requests while he explores all the different options it has.

His first mission is to locate vendor invoices. He searches for the gym's supplier of Immortazyne, snapping a picture of the phone number before casually sliding his phone back into his pocket. He taps on the keyboard and sets his features as if he's incredibly focused on the computer. About half an hour later, a young woman arrives for a job interview. Landon escorts her back to the office just as Frank announces that he's going out to buy a case of energy drinks since they're in danger of running out before the next shipment arrives.

Landon takes his parents' distractions as an opportunity to put his plan in motion.

Mumbling to his coworker that he's going to check the inventory, Landon turns and slips into the storage closet. Adrenaline rushes through him as soon as he's inside, behind the barrier of the door. When his eyes land on the clipboard, he adds his initials beside today's date. He'll do that every day that the gym is open.

Next, he pulls his phone out and punches in the number for the Immortazyne supplier. When a bored-sounding woman answers, he informs her that Infinity Fit is cancelling all future orders, that they've decided not to use the additive anymore. Her momentary surprise is quickly replaced by an indifferent, "Okay."

Maybe he can get Carter to play along and pretend that they're still adding it to the water. By the time his parents figure out that it's not true, they'll realize that they don't need it to run a successful business.

Returning the cell phone back into his pocket, he opens a box of straws. He pulls out the contents – two big clear plastic bags with hundreds of straws in each – and sets them on a rack. He places the Immortazyne box inside the empty straw box and strides out the door.

"Just throwing out an empty box," he calls over his shoulder to his coworker. "Be back in a minute." With a confidence fueled by following his conscience, he exits the brick building and rounds the corner to the dumpster behind the building. Raising the flimsy black lid, he tosses the box inside and returns to the entrance. After a trip to the restroom to wash his hands, he circles around to the front desk and gets back to work, refreshed and riding the high of doing the right thing. Even if his parents will never know.

TWO WEEKS LATER

"They'll probably send me home early again today," Carter says, shaking his head. "I just don't get it. Where is everyone? This place has been slow for a solid week now. It's never like this. If members don't show up, they don't need two of us at the desk."

"It is summer, maybe they're on vacation?" Landon shrugs, unconcerned. "It hasn't been that long. They'll be back."

"I guess . . . so you coming over to watch the game tonight?" Carter asks, grabbing a basket of clean towels to fold.

"Yeah, I'll be there by seven," Landon confirms, slipping a stack of class schedules into a clear acrylic holder on the counter.

The easygoing mood instantly shifts when a man in a dark gray suit breezes through the glass entrance doors. He carries an air of authority and clearly isn't here to exercise. Closer in proximity to the stranger, Landon greets the man and asks how they can help him. With the flick of his wrist, the man displays a golden shield-shaped badge.

"I'm Detective Walkins and I'd like to speak with the owner." The man's voice is confident and smooth. He's definitely not asking. He's stating what's going to happen.

"Sure, I'll get them," Carter says, turning away and heading to the office door. Landon eyes the detective curiously. Questions soar through his mind, but he's too stunned to ask any. Within a minute, Frank rushes out and greets Detective Walkins, leading him to the office and promptly closing the door.

"What the heck is that about?" Carter mutters.

"I have no idea," Landon answers.

The office's walls are too thick to hear any details of the conversation, but a few times the guys hear a man's voice rise. Landon's not sure if it's the detective or his father. Either way, intensity spills from the room as soon as the door swings open. Both Steph and Frank walk Detective Walkins to the door and exchange firm handshakes. As his parents stalk back to their office, Landon shoots them a questioning look. Steph shakes her head no, a silent message that they'll talk about it later. Unable to wait, Landon follows them, closing the door behind him.

"What was that about?" he demands.

"We'll talk at home, son," Frank says dismissively.

"I want to know now," Landon says, crossing his arms. "If I'm going to run a place like this, I need to understand what kind of scenarios might happen and how to handle them."

"Fine," Steph says. "Apparently the hospital had a slew of admissions, all of them presenting the same symptoms – intense headaches, lethargy, nausea, anxiety, even hallucinations. The doctors had never seen anything like this, just a bunch of people having the same symptoms at the same time. They started to consider if it was the start of an outbreak of some sort. The administrator analyzed the patient medical records and found one common denominator – when asked about their physical activity, they all claimed to be members here."

"How does that have anything to do with it?" Landon mutters, stepping backward toward the door, as if he could physically distance himself from the situation.

"The detective asked for a report of all of our members and their activity – when they swiped in and out of the gym, for the past month, so they can compare the data. We're going to run that information and send it to him," Frank explains grimly. "They're also sending in a health inspector to check our food preparation processes, perishable goods and water."

"It's worse, though," Steph adds. "One of them, Mr. Basker, is in a coma. He's been unresponsive for two days now." She squeezes her eyes shut as a tear rolls down her cheek. Frank rushes to her side and wraps his arms around her.

"You can't tell Carter, or anyone else," Frank says. "Just act like nothing's happening. We'll get the police anything they want. We haven't done anything wrong. All we've done is helped our members and I have no doubt we can prove that!"

Landon's shoulders drop as he heads for the door. His insides twist as his parents' words replay in his mind. *What if these people are going through withdrawal from the Immortazyne?* Mr. Basker is one of their oldest members. The man's got to be at least eighty. If he doesn't make it out of that hospital, Landon knows it will be his fault.

There's only one thing he can do to try to fix this. He never should have stopped using the additive so abruptly. It would have been safer to do it slowly, to wean people off it. He strides back to the front desk, keenly aware of Carter's intense gaze that follows his every move.

"What's going on?" Carter asks, his eyes shifting back and forth as if someone might be eavesdropping.

"Oh, it's just this top secret sting the police are doing," Landon says, relieved by how quickly the lie occurred to him. "They want to send in a few undercover cops. It's really to monitor some activity at surrounding businesses, nothing to do with the gym actually."

"Phew," Carter blows out a deep breath. "That's good. I was afraid there was something crazy going on and that I was going down with the ship."

"No, man, you're good." Landon feels his pocket, ensuring his phone is there. "Hey, I need a minute. Gotta call this girl from school. She won't stop texting me. I'm gonna go in the storage room for privacy." A pang of guilt slithers through Landon. When did lying become so easy?

Carter flashes a thumbs-up as Landon slips into the supply room. Once the door's closed, he shuffles through his pictures until he finds the one he took weeks ago, of the Immortazyne supplier. He types the phone number into his phone. His pulse quickens with each ring. Finally, a man answers. Before he can finish saying hello, Landon blurts out his reason for calling.

"Hi, someone recently cancelled our order of Immortazyne by accident and I need to get a shipment right away, like overnighted." The words tumble out of his mouth so quickly, he worries the syllables all run together.

"Well," the man starts, "we can get your information and add you to the wait list. This stuff is so in demand that we can't keep it in stock. We've got several weeks' worth of backorders."

Landon's posture slumps in defeat as his mind races to find a solution. "But we really need it, like as soon as possible. Isn't there anything you can do?"

The man chuckles. "Wish I could, but we need more time. I just can't keep it in stock. If I had any, I'd sell it to you. I mean, you must know how great it is since you're calling to get more."

"Yeah, it is. That's why I need more. We can't wait," Landon pleads, keeping his voice low and urgent.

"Oh come on now," the man says. "It's not like it's life or death if you have to wait a few months for your next shipment."

"Let's just pretend it is, okay?" Landon says nervously. "There's got to be something you can do for me." Sweat beads along his forehead as the temperature seems to surge in the storage room.

"Look, I can let you in on a little secret," the man says, dropping his voice to just above a whisper. "We're testing a new product, called Immortazyne Ultra. It's twice as strong as the original. It's not FDA approved or anything yet, but we've got some small batches in production. If you'd like to be a testing site, I think we can make that happen."

"We'll take it!" Landon says. "Please, send it as fast as you can!"

FAMILY SECRET

A SERIES OF RAPID, sharp knocks jolts Diane from the pages of her latest read, an engrossing horror page-turner. She glances at her watch – 3:33 p.m. – although checking the time doesn't provide any clue as to who's come to see her. She wasn't expecting any visitors today. She jumps when the pounding grows louder, more urgent.

Dropping the paperback on the sofa, she rushes to the door, swinging it open to see a uniformed police officer waiting on the other side. Nausea churns in her gut. His presence is a stark reminder of the recent parking ticket, tucked neatly under her windshield wiper, that she ignored. She went into town and overstayed the meter by six minutes. Six measly minutes that cost her thirty dollars. Well, not quite, since she didn't pay it. Her cheeks flush with heat as she internally reprimands herself for not taking care of it. Plastering a fake smile across her face, she greets the officer.

"Miss Briar?" the tall, slender man asks, watching her intently.

"Yes, that's me." She chews her bottom lip, anticipating a stern lecture or a fine as punishment for ignoring the ticket.

The officer slips the navy blue hat off his head, revealing a bristly buzz cut. He lowers the hat to his side as his features soften with pity. "I'm sorry to inform you that there's been an accident. A car accident. Your mother was driving and —"

Diane's knees buckle as all air rushes out of her lungs. The officer catches her and pushes through the front door, navigating to the closest chair. "I'm sorry, ma'am, I should have asked to step inside before I said anything."

She clasps her trembling hands together and tries to slow her rapid breathing. "Please go on." She doesn't want him to, but she has to know.

"Miss, I'm sorry but your mother didn't survive the crash. We're conducting an investigation to determine the cause. The accident was fairly minor, but the car caught on fire and she was trapped inside. We can't say for certain yet, but most times if there's a fire after such a minor collision, it's due to a defect in the electrical system."

The permanent sting of loss stabs Diane's heart. Her father died before she was born and now she's lost her mother. Her first thought is that she's an orphan, which is absolutely ridiculous for an adult in her thirties.

"Miss, the chaplain is on her way here to provide support." The officer's gaze and tone emanate sympathy.

Diane shakes her head as the first of many tears escape her. "No, please leave me alone. I just need to be by myself."

"Are you sure you're in the condition to handle this alone?" he asks. "I can leave but the chaplain can still come if you'd like."

"No." It's a barely audible whisper, but Diane rises and stalks to the door, pulling it open. The officer stands, places the hat back on his head and walks toward her. He hands her a business card as he passes by.

"Please call if you have any questions or change your mind about the chaplain. I'll be in touch when I have more information."

As soon as he passes through, Diane closes the door, locks it and sinks to the floor, allowing herself to collapse into a pile of misery.

THE NEXT DAY

Diane rolls up to the gray split-level house. Her childhood home is just as she remembers it – purple flowers bloom throughout the knee-high sage bushes standing guard on either side of the front door, which matches the stark black shutters with decorative half-moons carved out of the top left corner. When she was old enough to reach them, she loved running her finger along the smooth curve.

Everything about the house looks the same as it did back then – perfectly imperfect cracked siding, sagging front porch and the crumbling chimney. As Diane climbs the steps, a burst of wind rushes across the porch, sending the creaky old rocking chair into a gentle sway. A flash of lightning bursts across the sky moments before thunder cracks. Diane startles as the sound, like a giant striking a mighty hammer on a slate, pierces her ears. She rushes to unlock the door and slip inside just as a spray of fat, heavy drops pelt the ground.

As soon as she flips a light switch on, her heart aches. The familiar photographs, furniture and knickknacks are no match for the foreboding emptiness she feels. A rush of memories sweep through her, at war with the stark reminder that there won't be any new memories made here with her mother.

Unwilling to awaken emotions tied to other areas of the house, Diane climbs the stairs and follows the hallway to her old bedroom. Dropping her bag on the floor, she goes through the motions of washing her face, brushing her teeth and changing into pajamas. She climbs into bed, listening to the rain's steady beat as memories play through her mind.

Wrapped in the comfort of home, she drifts asleep as the thunder shifts toward its next target, its echoes growing more distant.

The next morning, Diane wakes to the grogginess of forgetting where she is and why she's there. Sadness washes over her when she remembers. *I've got to figure out what to do with Mom's house,* she thinks. *I could sell it and buy a small place without the constant reminder that she's gone, or I could ditch the apartment and move in here.*

She pushes the thoughts from her mind. One day at a time. One task at a time. Either way, she'll need to start going through the house and look for bills and anything else that needs to be taken care of. She dresses for the day and walks down the stairs, like she's done hundreds of times before.

Unsure where to start or what to do, she wanders into the kitchen. Peeking inside the cupboards, Diane grabs a box of cereal, a bowl and a spoon. The milk in the refrigerator is expired, so she eats it dry. In between bites, she pages through papers near the phone. A letter with a car manufacturer logo emblazoned at the top captures Diane's eye. It explains that her mother's car is part of a recall for defective sensors. *Maybe that caused the accident,* Diane wonders, thinking back to what the police officer said. She swallows any regrets for what may have been preventable and continues her search for anything that might need attention.

Her gaze shifts to the wall calendar. Familiar loopy cursive writing notes an appointment at the car dealership on Friday, the thirteenth. The little circle printed beside the date predicts a full moon. Her mother drew two dots and a curved line inside it, making a smiley face. Diane's gut clenches. If that appointment had been sooner, would the accident have ever happened? Pressing the heels of her palms to her eyes, she decides some mindless scrolling on her phone may help reset her thoughts.

She circles the kitchen, searching for the device. Normally it's within arm's reach but this whole trip has felt surreal since she got here; nothing is as usual. Realizing she didn't use her phone since yesterday, she grabs her keys and heads for the door. Clomping down the porch steps, she jogs to her car and eyes the phone sitting idly on the passenger seat.

Clutching the phone and slamming the car door closed, she spins on her heel and heads back to the house. Diane settles in the rocking chair and checks social media only to find the typical array of funny memes, news briefs and acquaintances' self-created drama. Relishing the gentle breeze and the soothing motion of the rocking chair, she relaxes. The view is way better than at her apartment. Here the farm fields seem to stretch to the horizon. Her gaze travels across row upon row of corn stalks swaying in the wind.

Suddenly, movement draws her attention to the front door. A small dark creature disappears inside the house just as she turns to look. Apparently the door didn't latch closed when she first came outside because it rests on its hinges, open about a foot wide. Jumping out of the rocker, she runs inside, searching for the small furry mass.

'Um, hello . . ." she calls, taking careful steps from room to room. "Who's in here?" Any small animal would be hard to get out – a raccoon, rabbit or a possum. She walks around, clicking her tongue as if calling a pet. This thing could be wild, she thinks. It could have rabies. As she wanders through the kitchen, her visitor appears.

A long-haired black cat prances around, its green eyes brimming with curiosity. It shows no fear, as if it belongs here. Diane's brow furrows as she tries to remember if any of the neighbors have a cat. She can't recall, and for all she knows, the people she knew could have moved away and been replaced by strangers. She bends down, outstretches an arm and makes a BSWSWSWSWS sound. The cat strides over to her, allowing her to stroke its fur. They both jump when a bolt of lightning strikes nearby. Moments later, rain strikes the windows in a downpour.

"Great, another storm," she sighs. "I'm not going out in this, so I guess you can stay for now. Once it stops, we'll need to see if anyone's looking for you." The cat twines itself around her legs as if accepting the offer.

"You know what?" she asks the cat when a thought pops into her head. "We had a cat years ago . . . his name was Salem . . . and Mom probably never threw out his bowls and litterbox. I bet they're still in the attic. Wanna come with me up there to look? Come on."

The cat follows her up the steps and into the dark, dusty loft. She snaps the light switch on and looks around. Boxes are stacked in every corner, along with an old mattress frame, a maroon luggage set and two large bookshelves. Cobwebs stretch from surface to wall. She's careful to avoid colliding with any webs or their eight-legged architects.

Although it's not what she came up here for, Diane wanders toward the closest bookshelf. It seems to radiate a warm, welcoming aura. Her eyes are drawn to the thickest book on the shelf. It rests dead center of the middle row. Its deep brown leather is smooth to the touch. She slides it off the shelf expecting it to flip open, but it's sealed by a silver clasp engraved with an ornate star. She runs her finger over it. It's beautiful. When she squeezes the clasp, it springs open.

The cat sidles up beside her, demanding a chin rub. She lowers her butt to the worn wood floor, resting the book on her lap so she can pet the cat with one hand and turn pages with the other. The title page is *Book of Shadows* with her mother's name written in loopy cursive below the title. Beneath that, it says Born: October 31, 1692.

Diane gasps. That would make her more than three hundred years old. Her mother had a sense of humor, but what an odd year to write as her birthday. Maybe she wrote that when she was very young and thought it was funny. It was probably a joke for anyone who found this journal, or whatever it is.

Shaking her head, she flips through the book, finding pages that appear to be recipes with ingredients like herbs, salt, feathers and rose petals. Setting the book aside, she rummages through other books on the shelf. She's drawn to one bound in a crimson cloth. The word *Journal* is embossed on the cover and surrounded by curling vines with leaves outstretched toward the edges. It was once gold foil and probably elegant, but now bits of the letters and leaves flake away with the slightest touch. She flips it open.

The first page says *Book of Shadows,* just like the first book. But this handwriting is stiff and dark. Whoever wrote it pressed hard. The only identifier is a first name – Ravenna. *Maybe it's a long-lost relative,* Diane wonders. *How else would it end up in our attic?* The pages detail the girl's life, from a simple, carefree childhood to a search for power. Hand-drawn sketches reference an amulet that has been passed down through generations to protect whoever possesses it.

When Diane replaces the journal on the shelf, the black cat crawls onto her lap and taps her hand.

"What is it? Are you telling me to find what we came up here for?" she asks. The cat hops to the floor and saunters toward the other bookshelf. It paws at the bottom shelf. Diane follows and bends down to see what's caught the cat's attention, hoping it isn't a mouse.

Thankfully, the cat isn't focused on any creature – dead or alive. A simple wooden box sits on the shelf. It's about the size of Diane's palm. When the cat presses its nose to the box, pushing it forward, Diane picks it up and cracks open the lid. A blue oval stone, strung on a chunky silver chain, rests on the black satin interior. As she turns it in her hand, the gem glints like a mirror. It looks exactly like the hand-drawn amulet in the book.

Diane stares at it, mesmerized, certain she can see her reflection in the jewel's angled cuts. A delicate silver wire wraps around the top of the stone, reinforcing its connection to the chain. It's more than beautiful. Without a thought, Diane slips the necklace over her head. As soon as it touches her skin, the stone begins to glow. A warmth spreads from her core to her limbs. Energy shoots through her like a barrage of lightning strikes.

As she's frozen in place, absorbing the amulet's powerful energy, the cat climbs into her lap and gently paws at her cheek. With all her being, she's certain that this feline is much more than a cat. Running her fingers over the soft raven-black fur, she lowers her chin to meet the cat's eyes and smiles.

"It's you, Mom, you came back to me." With a sly grin, she adds, "You never told me you were a witch. I guess I'm one now too."

ENTRAILS

PART 1

AH, THE APPALACHIAN TRAIL. Nearly every inch is bathed in natural beauty, from the sun-dappled paths to the rocky ridges to the lush emerald foliage. After traveling the world – so many countries, continents, small towns and big cities that I've lost track – I can say with certainty that the A.T. is far superior.

I'm on a continuous trek that began decades ago, with no ending in sight. You see, I simply follow the trail – two thousand, two hundred miles each way from start to finish. When I reach the endpoint, I begin again, reversing my path. It's a good life, if you can call it that.

Is it lonely? No, not in the least. I can choose solitude or socialization any time. I only choose socialization when need requires it. That need would be sustenance. I spend my time watching from the trees, from sunset to sunrise. You never know what, or rather who, the night will bring.

Given my simple lifestyle, I have the luxury of allowing my mood to guide each day. Sometimes I lounge around waiting for dinner to come to me. Other days I crave the thrill of the hunt. Either way, I've been around long enough to know what prey is worth my time. I rarely expend much effort. There's no need when they're so willing to engage.

"Hi, how's it going?" I ask when our paths converge. It's a mindless conversation starter, a gateway to the inevitable. It often triggers them to notice my most unique feature.

"Are your eyes purple?" Some openly question me while others lean closer to get a better look before working up the nerve to ask. I don't offer up any information. Consider it a subtle cue of who is in control, right from the start. If they want to know, they have to ask. Of course I'm courteous when I respond.

"A shade of it, yes." I don't bore them with technicalities – they're actually violet – nor do I thank them for noticing.

At this point, some of them step even closer, invading my personal space, wondering if I'm wearing special contact lenses. To that question, I always respond, "Who is there to impress along the trails? A bear maybe?"

That's when they'll laugh, or at least chuckle. That slight exhalation, which my heightened senses devour, confirms if they would be a good candidate to meet my needs. It's an unobtrusive way, especially when they're up close and personal, of gathering what I need to know. No sense in wasting my time if they're of no use to me.

What seems to perplex them the most is that a man – and a very handsome one at that, so I've been told – has violet eyes. It's obviously possible, but it's not the biggest difference between me and them.

By now, some will offer a first name and a firm handshake. They never seem to notice how pale my skin is, especially for someone out in the middle of nowhere and obviously living off the land. When it's my turn to introduce myself, I choose a name, not my own of course. Some days I'm Javier or Santiago, others I'm Carl or John. Who, and what, I am is irrelevant to them because they have no choice in what happens next.

If they are remarkable enough to pique my interest, I need only cross their path once and the dance begins. It becomes a matter of time, of my choosing, until their ultimate demise. That's how nature works. We're all part of the food chain. Although most refuse to believe who is at the top. Surprise: It isn't humans. *Is it cruel?* No. They treat each other far worse than anything I would ever do.

At least my intent is simple – they are sustenance. Nothing more, nothing less. Of course I can't consume every single human I come across. I'm not a glutton, and repeated disappearances would trigger a search for a serial killer. I avoid drawing attention, sacrificing any recognition of my power for freedom.

The only thing I truly need, truly crave, is food. A big meal can sustain my strength for days. Once I determine that someone is worth pursuing, my stomach steers the course. If it's been too long since I've last eaten, my instincts take over and I sneak up on them. I watch as they, perhaps, sit around a raging campfire. Drinking, talking, completely unaware of my presence. Like good prey. Easy prey.

I'll wait until one inevitably wanders into the darkness, searching for a place to relieve their bloated bladder. As soon as they're empty, I strike. Wrapping one arm around their waist and one around their throat, cutting off their air supply. Together, as one unit, we disappear into the shadows cast by the trees as the firelight grows more distant. When we've travelled a few miles away, I feed. By then, my prey's heart is pumping wildly, nearly driving me insane. Hunger and thirst fuel my steps. When the time is right, or I can't hold back any longer, I plunge my teeth into their throbbing neck.

After the frenzy, when my stomach is brimming with nourishment, I decide what to do with the limp shell of their body. If I'm feeling creative, I may slash them open, a perfectly straight line down their middle. It's like when a stage curtain sweeps open, but this one releases bulging, juicy entrails that spill out, puddling into a sloshy pile at my feet.

Millions of people hike part of the trail every year. It's easy to get away with some going missing while others can be staged as animal attacks. As long as I eliminate any evidence that I exist, or any witnesses, I can disappear in the blink of an eye.

My senses are impeccable. I usually smell them before I see them. In the decades I've spent on this trail, I've realized that most "hikers" have very little backpacking experience. Not the smartest move. Often, they are young adults intent on avoiding grown-up responsibilities or retirees searching for meaning amidst a peaceful ecosystem where animals outnumber humans.

Imagine my disappointment when the first approaching stranger of the evening is a young woman, probably in her early twenties, who must have bathed in the most pungent, floral scent to ever touch my nose. Not a natural, earthy scent but a harsh, overbearing, artificial odor. It burns my nostrils for several long minutes before she reaches me. I'd take the musky, sweet essence of animal scat to this any day.

While she's one I would merely throw a curt nod at and keep going, she stops directly in front of me on a narrow part of the path, blocking the way.

"Um, hi." She twists long strands of golden hair around a finger while shifting on her feet awkwardly. "I'm sort of lost." She glances behind her and then past me, to the trail ahead. "Do you know your way around here?"

Inwardly, I cringe. She's not my type, which means she's a waste of my time. And she's already annoying me. How is anyone *"sort of"* lost? You're either lost or you're not. Instead of showing my true reaction, I pretend to care. Slightly.

"I'm sorry to hear that. Where are you trying to get to?"

Instead of answering, her back straightens and she twitches with some sort of realization. *Oh great, here it comes.*

"Are your eyes purple?" She slips the baseball cap off her head and rises on her tiptoes, squinting as she draws closer. Her scent washes over me and I nearly cough to rid the stench from my airways. Clearing my throat, I stand tall, refusing to take a step back even though it's what I most want in this moment.

"They're violet actually, but never mind that." Yep, she's got to go. "I can point you in the right direction, but I need to know where you're headed."

"Wow, I've never seen violet eyes. They're just stunning, really." She tilts her head, mesmerized. Pungent Flowers. That's her name, at least in my mind. Although hopefully after this brief encounter, I'll never have to think of her again.

"Yes, thank you, anyway . . ." I turn my wrist around in the air. I've seen the humans do that to encourage someone to hurry up. Perhaps this will remind her to get to the point. Patience is not a virtue that I hold.

"Oh right, so if I could just get to the nearest town, I could call my friend to come get me and drive me to my car. I parked at the Hunters Run lot, but I have no idea where that is." She huffs out a big breath as if providing this information is somehow a strain. "I saw a butterfly back a ways. It was black with a bright orange line on each wing and white dots. It was so pretty. Anyway, I started chasing it to get a video and when it flew away, like too high for me to reach it anymore, I got all turned around. I found a trail, but I don't think this is the right one and now it's getting dark."

A butterfly? This moron got herself lost because she followed a butterfly? And because of that she needs my help. I could give her exact directions – follow this trail, in the opposite direction, for a quarter mile, then take the path when it branches off to the left, from there it's a straight shot. I'm certain she can't follow those simple directions on her own. As much as it pains me, other scents mingle with the air – promises of violence and harm. Not to me, of course, nothing I can't handle, but she's no match for the evil cloaked in darkness.

"I know how to get you back to that lot. Follow me, but stay quiet. There are lots of wild animals out here and we don't want to attract them." Besides that, I'd rather not hear any more about her adventures tormenting butterflies.

I brush past her, charging in the direction she just came from. She stumbles to keep up with my quicker pace. We travel no more than two hundred feet before her mouth starts to run again.

"So are you a local or are you hiking the whole trail?"

My irritation swells when she stumbles, crashing into my back. I steady her as she apologizes and brushes dirt off her pants. While facing her, I make another attempt to end any further conversation before it starts.

"I need to concentrate on where we're headed. As you can probably imagine, it's more difficult in the dark." Not really for me, but it seems like a good excuse. "So let's skip the chitchat for now. Focus on where you're stepping. You don't want to twist an ankle out here."

She mutters a dejected, "Fine," as we continue. I let my mind wander as a distraction from the acrid scent of her perfume burning my nostrils. The last time I fed was two days ago. It was about twenty miles from here. I came upon a middle-aged man and woman. Upon first glance, you'd think they were a couple. But I knew something wasn't quite right. Their scents mingled with stark contrast. I smelled fear, aggression, dominance and hatred.

As I neared the simple campsite they'd set up for the night, my eyes confirmed what my nose guessed. Three ragged red lines etched into his cheek must have been where she clawed in a fruitless attempt to escape. Her bound hands, wrapped in a zip tie, not a practical choice for hiking a rugged trail, which told me she didn't choose to be tied.

It reminds me of other similar situations I've come across. Sometimes the victim is gagged, with or without a face mask firmly in place to cover the restraint. I guess some people found a use for remnants of the pandemic.

Either way, I listen to their exchanges to confirm my suspicions. Don't want to interrupt some kinky role playing that I'm not invited to. The crickets and locusts insist on making their voices heard, but my heightened senses tune them out when necessary. Once I'm sure that my assessment is correct, and someone is being held against their will, I strike. Although humans may be taught otherwise, I like to play with my food.

I usually spring from one treetop to the next, quiet as a faint breeze in the night air, until I drop to the ground like a bullet taking aim. I like the shock and horror my entrance creates. My first priority is immobilizing the suspect, although they are not truly a suspect by that point – they're guilty. One swift uppercut to the jaw usually knocks them out. I let them fall where they land, whether it's on a sharp rock, a jagged log or a patch of exposed tree roots. That's the least of their troubles.

At that point, I free the victim. If they're tethered by a bungee cord, I slice it with a flick of my finger. Their terrified eyes somehow grow wider as a scream builds in their throat. I press a finger to my lips. This is when they notice my eyes. It actually calms them a bit – their brain shifts from panic to intrigue. But only for a moment. I know that scream is itching to release.

"Listen to me carefully," I say calmly, requiring some sort of acknowledgment. When their fear fades to a mild tremble, I continue. "I am not going to hurt you. I only hurt bad people." I gesture toward their former captor. They'll usually nod, still watching me as if I could turn on them at any moment.

"Stay down and stay quiet. I know you did not come here by choice. I will get you out of here and back to safety."

That's when they start to believe even while their hands tremble and their heart flutters like a bird beating against its cage.

"Are you strong enough to walk for a few miles?" Most of them nod feverishly regardless of how far I estimate they'd have to traverse. I doubt they even comprehend distance in their desperation to escape the personal hell this woodland became. "Go in that direction. In just under two miles, you'll come to a police station. Tell them what happened but say nothing about me."

This is when confusion twists their features. Sometimes they'll cock their head toward me, but they rarely verbalize the obvious question – why? I know a few have told police about me. They've put out rough sketches of a person of interest. When that happens, it's time to move on. With so many miles of trails, that's pretty easy. Taking advantage of their full attention, I give them one last instruction.

"Tell them a bear approached and you ran away. Take the zip tie, or bungee cord or whatever was used to restrain you, rub the cut edges against tree bark and then drop it there. Tell them you got it off yourself. I'll make it look like a bear took care of him." I jab a thumb in the air toward my next meal.

"Th-thank you." It usually comes out as a stutter as they back away, watching me as if I'm the one who did this to them. Either way, it's fine because it is time to feed and they're not invited to watch.

Once the victim runs away, their waning scent confirmation that the distance between us is growing, I take care of the captor – banishing them from their pitiful existence that thrives on harming others. I take my time, slowly draining every last drop of blood from their body until it's an empty husk. They deserve to feel the same fear they've inflicted on others.

Just as my memories run their course, we've reached the last leg of this trek. I stop. Of course Pungent Flowers, or so I've taken to calling her in my mind, isn't paying attention and slams into me. She rights herself and mutters an unapologetic "Sorry." When I'm certain she's paying attention, I provide the last set of instructions.

"There," I point in the distance, straight ahead. "See that clearing? This is a back entry point, but it will take you to the Hunters Run parking lot. You can't miss it." Although I don't say it, if anyone could miss something right in front of their eyes, I have full confidence it would be her.

A relieved smile parts her lips the moment her eyes land on the opening that leads to the parking lot. She nods, gaze fixed on her destination.

"As you can see, it's not far. Just keep going straight." I start to turn but freeze in place when her protest comes out as a whine. An irritating high-pitched whine.

"You're not coming with me? Don't you want to make sure I make it all the way there?" The smile drops into a sulk and she literally pouts. The solitude of the trees and insects sounds like heaven at this point. Or the closest I will ever get.

"Remember what I told you." It's not a question, nor a suggestion. It's a promise that she *will* keep. "Tell no one about me. You got lost and by some miracle found the way back to your car."

"But—"

I raise a hand in the air to stop whatever ridiculous plea she can think of. It makes no difference. "Go. I have somewhere to be." With that, I turn from her and stalk back toward my den. I will no longer entertain this woman's emotions. I've done more than I should have.

All the others I've helped have gladly run away from me, zipping in the direction I point them in. Far away from me and whoever terrorized them in these woods to begin with. The only good thing about it is that they probably won't ever come back. The experience proves traumatic enough that they may never step foot in the woods again.

If that's the case, it helps me remain anonymous. I prefer to be a myth, the stirrings of folklore. I should be a hero but if too many humans knew about me, they would twist my story into something evil.

What exactly makes me a hero? You see, the only blood I crave is savory, succulent. And that sort of blood only flows through the most vile members of society. The morally corrupt have the spiciest blood. Nothing else is worth my time. It certainly doesn't meet my tastes.

Pungent Flowers – her blood is bland. I could smell it, well, hints of it beneath the perfume she doused herself in. The people I save cannot comprehend just how lethal I am, yet they are completely safe with me. What flows through the purehearted is tasteless, unless you like drinking iron. And I don't.

It wouldn't truly quench my thirst. I'd much prefer a satisfying indulgence. Living in the woods isn't exactly a luxurious existence, but it does give me unlimited access to a fresh flow of food. And my senses delineate the tastiest morsels. In this sense, I'm doing humankind a favor. A kindness. I help rid the world of some of its worst occupants.

"You never told me your name!" she calls, a final attempt to breach the solitude I so desperately crave. Pretending I don't hear her, I continue on my way. But seconds later, it reaches me, like the breeze carrying a whisper. A realization. The hairs on the back of my neck rise. A new scent floats through the air, burning my nostrils.

Infatuation. Her infatuation, with me.

Yesterday's Tomorrow

Priya's gaze sweeps from room to room through the small Cape Cod's interior one last time. She commits every detail to memory. The worn brown couch with mismatched orange pillows. The tiny kitchen, where the refrigerator door collides with a chair if it isn't tucked beneath the table completely. She thought she'd spend the rest of her life in this house. Maybe in a sense that's true, because today is the last day of her old life.

Wandering to the kitchen table, Priya wiggles the thin platinum band off her finger and slides it across the smooth surface littered with crumbs and last night's losing lottery tickets. Good riddance, she thinks as the ring catches a ray of sunlight streaming through the window, as if it's bidding her farewell with one last wink. With shaking hands, she slips a tattered blue bag over her shoulder. Its frayed edges tickle her forearm as the bag's contents – a few changes of clothing and basic toiletries – bulge against the seams. After grabbing her keys, phone and purse, she charges through the front door without leaving a note.

Priya's stomach twists into knots as she drives to the bank. Her gaze shifts back and forth, from pedestrians to other cars, as if any random person she passes is watching, eagerly waiting to report her every move to Liam. It was too risky to withdraw the money ahead of time. That would have saved her a step this morning, but if Liam got some alert that she drained their account, there would be hell to pay. And he would collect it, with great pleasure.

She pulls into a parking spot and checks her reflection in the rearview mirror. Her eyes immediately land on the raised pink welt marring her left temple. Blowing out a sigh, she scrunches the shortest layers of her thick, raven-hued locks forward. If they hang just right, they'll cover the wound. It would be easier to hide if it were just a few days' old.

With a fierce sense of determination, Priya informs the teller that she wants to close the checking account. That $2,068 will have to be enough. It's all she has but if it can buy her a new life, it's a gold mine.

"Switching banks?" the teller asks, running a hand through her hair. When Priya blinks, startled by the question, the woman explains, "Anytime someone closes an account, we're supposed to ask if you want to provide any feedback on what we could have done better."

"Oh, nothing," Priya starts nervously. "I'm, uh, moving." She flashes a small smile that tugs at her lower lip, right where it split at the point of impact with Liam's fist. A swipe of scarlet lipstick easily disguises it. Just like a thick layer of foundation and a stroke of blush dulls the sensitive purple blotch circling her jaw.

The teller nods, checking a box on a paper before typing a few more commands on her keyboard. Within ten minutes, Priya has the cash in hand – her ticket to freedom. She merely existed for the last seven years, suffocated by Liam's constant need to know where she was and what she was doing. But soon it will all just be a memory that will fade a little more with each new day.

Realization fuels her steps, pushing her pace faster as excitement blooms within her. It carries her to the car, and she settles in for the two-hour drive. Before starting the engine, she searches the parking lot for anyone who might be watching. Of course Liam has no idea she skipped work today, yet paranoia tugs at her brain. She scans the other cars in the lot and the nearby buildings, searching for any indication that she's been followed.

Once she's satisfied no one is paying her any attention, she counts out three hundred dollars and shoves the folded bills into her pocket. She'll need money for basic supplies. Even if she has to live in her car for a while, it doesn't matter. It's better than living with him for one more day.

Nothing, or no one, can stop her now. Blazing down the highway, she blasts the radio, belting out lyrics she makes up when she doesn't know them. She rolls the windows down, laughing as the air current tosses her hair around with the force of a tornado. It will be a scraggly nest of knots by the time she gets to her destination, but it doesn't matter. Freedom is invigorating. And this is just the beginning.

When the robotic voice on her phone announces that she's reached her destination, she follows the last few commands – turning down a long, winding driveway that leads to an enormous two-story house. Now that she's arrived, anxiety weighs on her. She didn't take the time to thoroughly research this company. What if it's a scam? When your husband randomly checks your browsing history, every keyboard click is intentional, and has to be cleared before you turn the computer off.

But her only other option is to turn around and go right back to the life she hates. With him. She's done that twice before – gave up before she followed through with her escape plan. Squeezing her eyes shut and gulping down the lump in her throat, she decides that the third time is a charm.

After shifting the gear into park and turning the engine off, she glances around. Of course there's no way Liam could be here, he has no idea where she is, yet the thought is always there, like he somehow knows what she's doing. With a deep breath and a cleansing release, she exits the car and follows the curved path of brick pavers toward the massive home.

She charges toward the ornate white pillars that mark the entrance. After pressing the doorbell, she admires the goliath estate. The stone walls alternate in varying shades of brown, from light tan to deep mocha. About half the windows are standard rectangular openings, but the rest are graceful nooks that curve outward. They'd make the perfect reading perch for whoever is lucky enough to live inside. A moment later, a tall, thin man opens the door and greets her. His neatly cropped black hair is peppered with gray around the temples.

"Miss Fredrick, I presume?" The man extends a hand, which she accepts and shakes with a fake confidence she doesn't feel.

"Yes, but you can call me Priya." No need to correct him on the missus part since that is about to change. "And you're Mister Allister?"

"That I am." He steps beside the open door and sweeps an arm toward the interior. "Please come in."

Priya steps inside, pressing her lips together, swallowing any awe that threatens to spill out. Sparkling marble tile meets stark white walls that form the grand entranceway. Leafy potted plants stand at attention, evenly spaced between elaborate paintings hung in thick gold frames. Each canvas captures a sailboat in the throes of a storm at sea. Priya's mesmerized by the deep blues of the water that morph into raging gray clouds on a foreboding black horizon.

She forces herself to stop gawking when the man closes the door and asks her to follow him. She catches glimpses of the luxury surrounding them as they walk. A staircase with wrought-iron railings winds its way to the floor above. A cluster of mirrors overtakes a wall. There must be a dozen of them in varying sizes – some as big as her torso and others the size of her palm. Each one is the same shape – a golden sun with sharp fingers, its rays, reaching out in every direction. The rounded center holds each mirror. Priya watches her reflection flow through the man-made constellation as they pass.

Just before the kitchen, with its black marble countertops and matching island, Mr. Allister stops at a door. He leads her through it, to a lower level. It's obviously a basement, but it's just as beautiful as the glimpses she saw of the first floor. They wind around a plush burgundy sectional that faces a movie-theater-size screen and approach an area sectioned off with half-walls.

Mr. Allister turns into the space and takes a seat behind an enormous mahogany desk. When he motions to a set of high-back chairs on the opposite side, Priya slides into one, the pliable cushion adjusting to her shape. A single manila folder rests on the shiny wood surface.

'We just have some paperwork to finalize and then we can proceed with your . . . journey." As he opens the folder and flips through some papers, Priya slides the small stack of bills toward him. He looks from the money to her before a frown tugs at the corners of his lips. It's obviously less than he was expecting. Much less.

"It's all I've got," she says, trying to keep her voice steady. *Not like you need it anyway,* she thinks.

His gaze rakes over her as if he's truly seeing her for the first time – from her stringy, scraggly hair courtesy of driving with the windows down, to the bruises marring her face. Pity flashes in his pale blue eyes and his face pinches slightly.

"It's fine." He picks the bills up as if they're covered in rat feces and shuffles them to the bottom of the paperwork. "So how did you hear about us?" he asks, changing the subject.

"Just a random online search," she says. "I was looking for . . . options to start over."

"I hear that a lot," he says, taking a pair of glasses out of his shirt pocket. He slides them on before handing her a few papers from the folder.

"This is my standard contract. It basically says that you are paying me for a service, I will provide that service and we will part ways. It doesn't go into too much detail. As you can surely imagine, most would never believe this arrangement is legitimate, so I find it best to keep the paper trail, along with our online presence, vague. It's as simple as you get what you want and I get what I want."

Without breaking eye contact, he reaches into a drawer, snatches a pen and offers it to her. She takes it, turning it over to admire the fountain pen's sleek design. Its sharp golden point is ready to release a steady stream of ink. With untamed eagerness, Priya presses the tip to the paper, pressing so hard that her name leaves an indentation in the paper's fibers. She hands the pages back to Mr. Allister, who slips the agreement into the folder and files it in the desk drawer.

"Well, now that that's taken care of," he says, planting his elbows on the smooth surface and joining his hands, "how far did you want to go?" Raising his scruffy gray eyebrows, he waits.

"How about twenty years?" Priya twists a lock of long dark hair around her finger and chews her bottom lip. This is the fun part. Just the idea of being twenty-five again sends a rush of adrenaline through her.

"I don't recommend more than ten years. This is a lot for the human body. It's not exactly natural. The shorter the . . . trip . . . the safer it is," he explains, folding his hands.

"Fifteen," she says, crossing her arms as she leans back in the chair. "We'll both compromise by five years."

He holds her gaze, silently challenging her words. When she sits up straighter, he relents.

"This is the farthest I've ever sent anyone. If you accept all the risks, then I guess we have a deal."

"I do." Ten years isn't enough. Even though they weren't married yet, she and Liam would be dating. But fifteen years ago, they hadn't met yet. She'd still go to her cousin's wedding, just like she did back then, but this time she'd steer clear of the handsome groomsman with curly dark hair and vibrant green eyes. She'd ignore the compliments and attentiveness that would slowly transform into insults and ultimatums. Maybe she could meet someone better that same night.

"Okay, then. It's your choice." Disappointment darkens his features, but it won't change her mind. She's ready to face any risks if it means escaping her husband forever. She's certain nothing could be worse than Liam's temper. Besides, her first two attempts to leave him failed miserably. This time it has to work, even if it means taking a bigger risk, believing in the unbelievable.

Mr. Allister explains that she'll enter the machine and the door will seal shut so that the energy it creates does not seep out. She should expect to feel some jostling and a change in the air, but it should all be minimal. The whole process should take about thirty minutes. When it's complete, the door will slide open and it will be safe for her to come out. She will be in this same house. He cannot guarantee if anyone will be there when she arrives. Either way, he suggests she sneak out as quickly as she can.

Priya shakes her head as he talks, agreeing with every instruction and warning. When he gives her the chance to ask any final questions, she asks only where the machine is. With that, he rises and stands before the bookcase on the wall opposite his desk. Its eight shelves are packed with books, many of them so high that Priya would need a stepping stool or small ladder to reach them.

Mr. Allister fishes a small box from his pocket and depresses a button. It reminds Priya of a garage door opener. She startles when the bookcase rumbles. It slowly, steadily shifts to the left, sliding along a track, revealing another room behind it. He strides through the opening and into a small, square space with a white igloo-shaped dome big enough to hold two or three adults.

The only other item in the room is a counter-height control panel. The flat desk-like surface is covered with buttons, switches and knobs. Mr. Allister types a few keys – it must be a code – and a screen, embedded in the wall, lights up. After a few more taps, the thick door to the igloo-shaped pod opens, lowering itself forward until it rests on the floor. A sharp burst of air rushes past Priya, ruffling her hair in its wake.

"Okay, it's all clear," Mr. Allister says. "You can go inside and step away from the door. It will just take a few minutes to adjust the settings and then you'll be off. I wish you a safe trip and a better tomorrow."

"Thank you," she answers, stepping into the pod. The interior is all white and cushioned, like a ball with bubble wrap lining. An etched honeycombed pattern runs over it. Everything about it feels sterile, from the antiseptic smell to the bright lights beaming from the padded wall.

Priya sucks in a breath as the doors slide closed with a whoosh, sealing as if they'll never part again. Her heart flutters. For the first time she wonders what she's gotten herself into. What if this guy's a lunatic? She's here alone, didn't tell anyone where she was going, and now she's trapped in some igloo in a stranger's basement.

A swirling buzz rises, as if she's inside a giant beehive and hundreds of stinging insects circle, churning in a continuous motion around her. She wraps her arms around herself, just in case anything pokes out and touches her. Smoke fills the pod. She coughs but the smoke has no taste, no scent. It doesn't even tickle her throat. The pod rocks back and forth as if it's teetering on an edge. It jumbles her bones and rattles her brain. Throbbing blooms in her ears. Sweat beads along her hairline.

Just when she thinks the contents of her stomach are about to force their way out, the rocking slows and the smoke seeps away. She watches as every last drop of it is sucked into the cracks and crevices between the padding. She runs her hands over her face, wiping away the sweaty sheen.

As she focuses on taking deep breaths, the door cracks open and slowly drops to the floor just as it did when she first saw this thing. This time she feels the air being pulled from the space as it's sucked out. She inhales a few more deep breaths before cautiously emerging from the pod. The lights are out, and darkness stretches to every corner of the small room. She pats the wall until her hand lands on a switch. The lights reveal that she's in the same basement she started in. And it looks the same as it did before her journey started.

Her stomach churns with fury as she considers what this probably means. Other than literally being shaken up, she doesn't feel as if she's traveled through time. She decides that if this didn't work, she's getting her money back and buying a one-way ticket to a tropical island. She wonders if she should have done that from the beginning. No, she thinks, she doesn't want to just start over. She wants a fresh start, one that erases parts of her past. If she never met that sorry excuse for a husband, her life would be a million times better.

She pads up the stairs, retracing the path she followed when she first arrived. When she reaches the top of the steps, Priya peers into the kitchen. Her spirit deflates when no one's there. She turns toward the front door. As soon as she can get her money back, she's leaving. But she needs to find someone in order to do that.

"Hello, is anyone home?" she calls as she wanders down the hallway. She stumbles when she catches her reflection in the wall of mirrors. Standing directly before the biggest one, she leans closer to it. Crow's feet sprout from the outer corners of her eyes. Pronounced laugh lines are etched at the corners of her mouth. Dark circles droop below her eyes. A fresh wave of nausea threatens to relieve her stomach of its contents.

"What did you do to me?" Her unanswered cry echoes through the empty house.

She runs to the front door and yanks it open, calling out, "Is anyone here?" Dropping her head into her hands, she struggles to figure out what to do. After several minutes of exasperation that yields exactly no ideas, she opens her eyes, spying a rolled-up newspaper on the sidewalk. Stumbling over, she picks it up and unfolds it, immediately scanning the date in the top right corner. Bile rises in her throat. It's exactly fifteen years later. Mr. Allister sent her forward in time, not back.

Her jaw drops as she reads the front-page headline, "Mystery Deepens: Missing Beneficiary of Lottery Winner Sparks Nationwide Search." It's the top story, practically jumping off the page. Beside it is a photo of her aged but smiling husband, holding a gigantic cardboard "check" for $8.8

million payable from the state lottery. A smaller inset picture of their wedding day flaunts the happiness they once shared.

She skims the article, unable to sort her jumbled thoughts to fully comprehend what's happening. Slowly, critical details bubble to the top of her consciousness. Liam won millions. The last of his immediate family passed before him. As his wife, Priya would be the sole beneficiary of his estate, but no one's been able to find her.

Until now.

Prayer Circle

"WELCOME, LADIES. IT'S SO good to see you today," Grace calls out as the last members of their weekly group take their seats. She circles the room to the coffeemaker and fills a chipped green mug with the fresh brew. After dumping two packets of sugar and a dash of creamer into it, she finds her seat at the head of the table. Not that there's really a main, or head, seat at a round table, but Grace commands order, and the others look to her to lead them. She decides when the group will begin and when it's time for them to move on to the next topic. It's one perk of being the pastor's wife – she's automatically in charge of any activity or event that she attends.

She scans everyone around the table to ensure any side conversations are extinguished. She won't start until she has their full attention. Surprise sends her pulse racing when she spots an unfamiliar face among the group. The girl must be in her late teens or early twenties. Her raven black hair hangs just past her shoulders, in sharp contrast to the other attendees' practical perms in varying shades of gray.

"It looks like we have a new participant, so let's start by going around the table and introducing ourselves. Just your first name and what you like best about our quaint little town." Grace flashes a broad smile as she meets everyone's eyes. "I'll go first. I'm Grace and I love our sense of community. You can't find that in a big city." She beams with pride as the usual group members introduce themselves and compliment the church or the neighborhood. Finally, it's the young woman's turn.

"Hi, I'm Elisa." She raises her hand in a half-hearted wave as her eyes shift from person to person. "I guess what I like most about this place is that my family's here."

"Well, we're glad to have you, Elisa. Now, let's get down to business, the reason we came together today," Grace says before turning her attention to the wooden box at the center of the table. She reaches out and slides it closer. The deep walnut finish is cold and smooth to the touch. The words "Prayer Box" are etched across the front in large cursive letters. White doves are painted on the top and sides, their wings spread in a sweeping flourish. A slit, the size of a stick of gum, is carved into the top so parishioners can anonymously drop notes explaining their prayer requests inside.

Sometimes the notes are lifelines for help in paying bills, finding a job or even a life partner. Every now and then a younger parishioner gets their hands on the box and stuffs a note inside asking for a baby brother or sister. Or maybe to get rid of a brother or sister.

Grace fishes a solid gold cross keychain out of her pocket and slides the single key dangling from it into the lock. "Now, let's get to work, ladies. For those who haven't been here before," she casts a pointed glance at Elisa, "members of our congregation drop prayer requests in this box throughout the week. We gather every Saturday to read the notes and pray for them. Never underestimate the power of prayer." A tight smile tugs at her cheeks, accentuating the wrinkles around her mouth.

Elisa slowly raises her hand.

"We're not in school, dear, you can speak freely." Grace says tersely, trying to hold back her annoyance. This girl is completely upending their routine. It's always exactly the same and it works. Perhaps if she'd just sit back and let the adults run things, they could make some actual progress.

"Um, okay," Elisa starts, her gaze shifting around the room. "I saw this on the church calendar and thought maybe people could come to ask for the group to pray for something. Does it have to be in writing . . . in that box . . . for the group to pray about it?"

Grace pinches her lips into a tight line. Just as she's about to respond, explaining that the group follows a process and cannot stray from what works, one of the longtime church members interrupts.

"Well, sure, honey," Thea says, adjusting her glasses. "You go right ahead and share your troubles with us. I'd say that's just as important as what's on some slips of paper. They're pretty much the same thing every week anyway."

Grace's darkened gaze lands on Thea, who ignores her. Before Grace can protest, the others chime in with their agreement, either muttering a simple "yes" or nodding their heads. Grace blows out a deep breath. Fine, she thinks, the girl can share whatever she thinks is so important, we'll say a quick prayer and then she can leave. She's never come to Prayer Circle before, and she probably won't be back.

Elisa nervously pushes her curly black hair behind her ears before dropping her hands to her lap. With her head down, she starts slowly, her voice just above a whisper. "Something . . . something weird's been going on."

As Grace opens her mouth, about to snap that she's already seen and heard enough theatrics, Katharine pulls her chair closer to the girl and drops her palm on top of Elisa's trembling hand, saying, "It's okay, honey, go ahead."

Elisa blinks rapidly, her lower lip quivering. She squeezes her eyes shut and whispers, "I think something is . . . haunting me."

Gasps echo throughout the room as shock spreads among the group.

"What do you mean, honey?" Katharine asks gently.

Elisa wipes away the tears forming in her eyes and inhales a deep breath. "My friends and I went to the old Archer farmhouse, you know, the one by the cemetery?" She looks around the room to make sure everyone's following. It takes all of Grace's willpower not to roll her eyes.

"That old, abandoned property in the valley," Thea mutters, confirming what they all know.

"Yeah, well, we went there and we were just being stupid. My boyfriend has a YouTube channel and he was filming us just going through the house and looking for anything interesting." Her gaze focuses on the door, as if she's in a trance, recalling the memories. "There was this one closet we opened and a burst of cold air came rushing out. It blew our hair around, even gave me goosebumps. It was like that door was just waiting to be opened, like pressure had built up behind it. It was so strong. It kind of freaked us out and we all ran out of there so fast."

"Well, at least no one got hurt," Katharine says. "By the looks of you now, you got out of there just fine."

"But I think, I think . . . something came with us." With these words, Elisa trembles in her seat. "That was two days ago and ever since it happened, I've been seeing weird things."

Grace crosses her arms. This girl must be in the drama club at school, she thinks, silently willing their guest to quit monopolizing the conversation.

"What kind of things, sweetie?" Thea encourages the girl.

"When I . . . when I look in the mirror." Elisa's lips form a thin line as she shudders with a sob she's unsuccessfully trying to hold back. Katharine scooches closer and wraps a comforting arm around the girl's shoulder. Elisa pulls a deep breath in through her nose before continuing. "My reflection is distorted. There are just black holes where my eyes and mouth are, and my hair is stick straight and white as snow."

Another round of gasps cuts through the air, like dominoes tumbling one after another, fueling the group's shared horror.

"All right, that's enough!" Grace booms, startling everyone in the room. "I don't know what your problem is, young lady. You've probably never spent a day of your life in church before, but today you show up and waste our time by sharing some crazy story as if you have a real problem." She picks the prayer box up with both hands and shakes it as her pent-up anger bursts free.

"I bet you wouldn't know a real problem if it slapped you in the face, young lady, and I will not idly stand by while you mock what we do. My husband is the pastor of this congregation and when he isn't here, I can surely speak on his behalf. He would not tolerate this attention-seeking behavior. Prayer circle works but it's only for believers."

She taps her pointer finger on the table with each syllable to solidify her point. "Our group offers support for real problems, not stories that people make up for attention."

Elisa's cheeks flush crimson and her brown eyes shoot open wide before she bursts into tears and drops her face into her hands. As the other ladies watch the scene unfold, their eyes narrow at Grace while those closest to Elisa rush to comfort the girl.

Incredulous, Grace shakes her head. *They can't possibly believe this girl,* she thinks. *If they do, they're a bunch of fools. Gullible fools. They should be ashamed of themselves for entertaining such nonsense in a place of worship of all places.*

As Katharine and Thea talk to Elisa in hushed tones, one of the other ladies, Sadie, raises her voice. "This young lady was brave to come here and ask for help, and that's exactly what we're supposed to do – help people. But instead, Grace, you choose to berate her?"

Sadie points a wrinkly, pale finger at Grace. "We've always been told to welcome newcomers with open arms, and you have been anything but welcoming. I think we should form our circle right now and pray! We'll pray for Elisa to find peace and stop whatever is happening to her. And we'll pray for Grace to grow in empathy. We've heard enough accusations. Let's focus on doing good and helping each other."

"I agree." One by one, all the other ladies chime in. Pursing her lips, Grace takes her seat. *They'll see*, she thinks. They'll all realize how stupid they're being and then she'll let them grovel. She'll show them just how compassionate she is by accepting their apologies.

"Let us join hands, ladies, and close our eyes," Katharine starts the circle, which is normally Grace's role. Fury burns in her gut as she firmly grasps the outstretched hands on either side of her. She closes her eyes and drops her head to her chest, silently vowing to maintain control over her emotions. As they pray in silence, Grace's thoughts run wild – of how she'll tell her husband all about how she was betrayed today. He'll surely know how to handle this act of mutiny.

When everyone opens their eyes, the signal that they are ready for the next prayer, Grace empties the box and flattens the small jumble of papers on the table. She reads each one before pausing so the group members can silently add their own intentions and help amplify the prayer. After a short time, they finish the last request.

The weekly gathering typically ends with amicable chatter, but not tonight. Instead the ladies slowly disband, filtering out of the room in small groups, some of them rushing to escort Elisa out. Grace focuses on gathering her belongings and locking up the prayer box. She barely acknowledges any goodnights muttered to her in passing.

Eager to avoid walking out with anyone, she stops at the restroom to rinse out her coffee mug. She flips on the lights and heads straight for the sinks, turning the hot water on. When she glances up, terror races through her. The mug in her hand crashes to the floor, shattering into a dozen pieces.

The wrinkles, the glasses are still there but dark, hollow pits sit where her eyes should be. Her mouth is an empty hole of nothingness and her graying hair is white as a ghost. It's exactly what Elisa described, and Grace has a strong suspicion that the girl doesn't have to worry about it anymore.

ENTRAILS, PART 2

ON WHAT SHOULD BE just another night, I'm ripped from my slumber, unsure if it's the stench or the noise that reaches me first. Perhaps they dually assault my senses at the same time. I'd recognize that stink anywhere. Pungent Flowers is back in my woods. And even though she'd never find my nest, her presence intrudes upon my cave, reverberating all the way to the farthest back wall. It's an unwelcome invasion even if it isn't her physical presence.

Even in the distance, her heart flutters like a tiny winged creature beating against its cage. It's a sound I've heard many times, mostly just after I've pounced upon an unsuspecting meal. This time it wouldn't be so unnerving if it weren't for the putrid smell. She must douse herself in a combination of chemicals that is supposed to conjure nature. Instead it fills the air with a thick cloying scent that could scorch nostril hairs.

Against my better judgment, I rise and stalk to the cave's entrance. Just as I suspected – daylight is waning. It must be late afternoon. Even if I wanted to, it would be pointless trying to go back to sleep. That awful scent clogs the air, and every step she takes sounds like a horse clomping down the trail. Just when it seems she can't draw any more attention to herself, she starts calling out, "Hello! Is anyone out here?" Then, much quieter, she mumbles to herself, "Where's the tall, dark stranger I met last week?"

Evil lurks in these woods. Hints of it pass through the overbearing scent Pungent Flowers emits. And if she keeps yelling, it will find her. While I'd rather not engage, I can't exactly stand by and let an innocent woman suffer simply because she's annoying. And lacks common sense and basic intelligence. Her only redeeming quality is that she recognizes that I am far superior to other men and she craves seeing me again. It's difficult to fault her for that.

Under the weight of resolve – why am I compelled to do what's right? – I trek through my private path and emerge from the lush emerald foliage. I choose to enter the trail behind her. She startles when she turns, the faint rustling of brush drawing her attention, and her eyes open wide when they land on me.

"It's you!" she squeals. Literally squeals in whiny, high-pitched delight. She closes the gap between us in three clumsy steps, bumping into me when she attempts to stop before infringing upon my personal space.

"Yes, and that's you, but we both already knew that." I pause, hoping my curt tone will offend her. When it fails to wipe the giddy smile off her face, I try to reason with her. "It's getting dark, you'd better start heading home."

"But I finally found you! The whole reason I came out here was to find you again." The goofy grin crinkles the corners of her eyes, and I sense the genuine delight she feels over this accomplishment. Unfortunately for her, I don't feel the same.

"Well, you found me. Good on you." I wrap my fingers around her elbow and tug her along the path with me. "But let's get you out of here before you can't find your way out again."

She digs her heels into the dirt. "No! I want to talk." She swipes a wisp of golden hair away from her eyes. "I didn't really get a chance to thank you for helping me last time."

"No need for thanks." Once again, I try to herd her along the trail. "You getting to safety is really thanks enough for me." Although using less perfume would also be a welcome gift.

She tugs her elbow from my grasp and crosses her arms, sulking. "Why do you want to get rid of me so bad?" she asks, hurt reflecting in her brown eyes. "I went to a lot of trouble to hunt you down!"

"This isn't the best place for you," I answer coolly. "Especially when the sun goes down. Scary things come out at night around here."

She rolls her eyes and huffs out a breath. "You know what I think?" She doesn't wait for me to answer. "I think you're scared. We have a connection. I can feel it and I think you can too, but you're scared of it. Don't you believe in love at first sight?" She stomps her foot and raises her thin arms in the air.

A deep grumbling laugh starts at the pit of my stomach and rumbles out my throat. "No, not exactly." Embarrassment flushes over her porcelain cheeks and her gaze drops to the ground. After a moment of charged silence, she aims a death glare my way.

"Fine. If you could just show me the way out of here, we can talk more on the way."

"Fine." Maybe I can tell her I need quiet, like the last time, to focus on where we're going. "Which way did you come from?"

She turns around, scanning our surroundings. Pressing a pointer finger to her mouth, she admits, "I'm not really sure."

Oh here we go again. I swear this woman could not be any more frustrating. I'm a little farther south on the path than I was last week, so we likely need to take a different route.

"Tell me, did you cross a bridge to get here?" As soon as the words leave my mouth, her posture straightens.

"Yes! Yes, I crossed a bridge." She smiles again, obviously proud of herself. Never mind she shouldn't even be here and because she's here, she requires my help. Again.

"Okay, follow me." I turn from her and charge down the path, not waiting to see if she's following or keeping my pace. The sooner I can get rid of her, the sooner I can find tonight's feast. I scent depravity in the air tonight – viscous and savory. My stomach reminds me that it's been a few days since it was last satisfied. The anticipation pushes each footstep faster, which prompts Pungent Flowers to complain.

"You're going too fast!" she whines. "My legs aren't as long as yours and if you want me to keep up, you need to slow down!"

I turn toward her, sending a scathing look her way. She crosses her arms and raises her eyebrows as if she's expecting me to say something – an apology perhaps? This girl really is delusional. I press my lips closed, choosing silence rather than encouraging more conversation. Facing forward again, I continue along the path, careful not to walk faster than her short legs can carry her.

When we reach a narrow part of the trail, I find my footing on a few smooth, flat stones. Before she even raises her leg, I sense an impending injury – possibly a sprained ankle. That's the last thing I need right now. In the blink of an eye, I spin around and catch her mid-air before she plants that foot down on what I know will be a misstep. Her mouth drops open and her eyes widen as her pupils dilate ever so slightly.

"Wha- what are you doing?" She runs a hand through her hair and watches me pointedly. I sense that she's taking this as a sign of my nonexistent interest in her.

"I knew that was a rough patch of rocks. I just didn't want you to fall." I immediately regret my response because a smile blazes across her cheeks and her heartbeat quickens. Pride radiates from her like a hummingbird performing a courtship display, diving through the air to show off its speed and agility.

"So you *do* care about me?" She chews on her bottom lip as elation blooms within her.

"Look, I don't know what you think could happen between us, but I assure you that it won't." It's time to break the spell, regardless of how harsh I must be. Whatever she thinks she sees in me is strictly on the surface. I've given her no reason to believe that I have any interest in her whatsoever. "Now I'd appreciate if we could just walk in silence. I'll get you back to your car and then I ask that you never come back here again."

Her nostrils flare as her fury grows. Red-hot anger reaches toward me like spindly claws outstretched. "Fine!" she barks.

"Let's just part ways right now and you'll never have to see me again!" Before I can respond, she brushes past me in a streak of crimson. She must be perspiring because the floral scent of her perfume grows stronger, knocking me back a step to avoid her leaving any trace of it on me.

She takes off, running away from me in some ridiculous protest. Fine by me. I'll still follow her, at a slight distance, and make sure she makes it out of here safely. It's even better than the alternative since now I don't have to argue with her or avoid conversation.

Her clomping footfalls, accompanied by audible sobs, echo through the trees. This can't be over soon enough. It makes me consider my own escape. If I feed tonight, I can leave this area first thing tomorrow evening. And forget just proceeding to a different section of the trail, I need to put distance between me and this place. Perhaps Europe will be my next stop. The good old E1 hike. It's far enough away, and long enough, that the probability of coming across Pungent Flowers ever again is less than negligible.

Envisioning myself in complete isolation thousands of miles from here, I can't help but smile. Just as quickly, it slides away as a shriek slices through the night. A loud creak and sharp snap chase the scream. Seconds later a crash erupts. It sounds like branches are ripping and stones are tumbling. A low moan reaches my ears just as the combined scent of terror and pain fill my nose.

Faster than a human could ever move, I run. My senses lead me not forward, but down. I tear through the trees and bushes, moving so quickly it probably doesn't even leave any indication that someone's passed through. When I reach a clearing at the bottom, the delicious aroma hits me like a wall, nearly knocking me off my feet. Blood. Refreshing, luscious, exquisite. My eyes hone in on her immediately. Pungent Flowers floats face-down in the water. Remnants of the bridge bob around her. It must have collapsed, at least part of it, and dropped her into the creek. It can't be more than a foot deep right now, which means the unwelcoming rocks beneath the surface would have broken her fall.

I turn her over to search for signs of life, but again I'm temporarily frozen, unable to react. Her scent. It's different. The awful, overbearing perfume must have washed away. Now I smell warmth, love, belonging. Centuries-old tales flash through my mind. All those stories weren't just whispers in the dark, they were accounts of vampires in history that found their one true love, their death link, because they were destined to spend eternity together. Their connection was sealed by the instant recognition of each other's scent, like no other they'd ever come across, confirming their perfect fit.

Shaking myself from the memories, I focus on the one fate delivered to me. I scoop Pungent Flowers in my arms and carry her to the bank. She's like a limp rag doll, her limbs and head swaying with each step I take. Dropping to the rocky edge that meets the water, I cradle her in my arms. Her head lolls to the side and rests on my chest. Blood streaks through her golden hair. Her eyes are empty voids, open but unseeing. Blood no longer pulses through her veins. A faint thumping resonates in her chest, but I know it's a false hope. The human heart can continue to beat even after death, if only for minutes.

She's gone. I'm certain of it. At the realization, an unexplainable sadness sweeps through my body, all the way to my trembling fingers. The sharp sting of loss pierces my unbeating heart. There is no saving her life, but I may be able to grant her an eternal afterlife. With me.

Instincts take over and I sink my fangs into her neck. Until now, the act has always been fueled by violence, domination and satiation. This time it's an act of compassion. Though I never believed this kind of connection truly existed, a rush of warm liquid flows through the hollows of my fangs. It's not of my control, it's an automatic response as nature takes its course. Immediately my energy mingles with hers, filling her with my power, my entire being. It must be how the connection is sealed.

As I gulp down her blood in the exchange, a glorious warmth spreads through me, like honey – thick and comforting. It makes everything I've tasted before seem like fast food compared to a five-course gourmet meal. I'd gladly lap up every last drop, but I don't know if it will harm her and it's not worth the risk.

When I think she's had enough of my lifeblood, I retract my canines gently and stroke her cheek as I wait for her to wake. Nearly an hour later, her leg twitches. Soon after, her hand clenches into a fist. Then, with a burst of breath and wide eyes, she starts convulsing. Holding her tighter, I speak soothingly and smooth the hair away from her face.

Slowly she seems to regain control of her movements. When her narrowed eyes focus on me, a soft smile tugs at her lips. She remembers me.

"You were right," I whisper, stroking her cheek. "We do have a connection and now we have eternity to enjoy it."

WISHING HELL

"FOUR HOURS? YOU SERIOUSLY wanna drive four hours when we can just hike around here?" Kali asks, slumping into the passenger seat.

"Just trust me," Reina says, glancing at her friend before sliding her gaze back to the road. "There's something really special at this place. It's totally worth it, and if you don't like it, lunch is on me today. Besides, have I ever steered you wrong before?"

"Well, there was that date you set me up on with your friend Bob. I'll never forget that disaster, as much as I'd like to." Kali crosses her arms, but the smirk playing across her face betrays her feigned anger.

"Then consider this my official attempt to make amends." Reina smiles broadly, flicking a wave of curly dark hair behind her shoulder. "Pretty sure you'll be thanking me the whole ride home!"

"Fine," Kali concedes. "I'm picking an expensive place for lunch though!"

"I don't think that will be a problem, in fact I'm certain it won't be." Reina giggles to herself as if she's made a joke. "So, Miss Soon-to-be Published Author, how's that manuscript coming along?"

The miles pass by quickly as the friends chat about the mundane aspects of the past week, which focuses mostly on complaining about their jobs.

"So you haven't really made any progress on the book, then?" Reina asks, flashing a side eye at her best friend.

"No." Kali shakes her head as the word slips past her lips. "Work is so crazy, I'm putting in time in the evenings just to keep up. It's sucking up all my writing time."

"Sounds like maybe you need a new job," Reina mutters. "One that isn't as demanding so you actually have time and brain power left at the end of the day to do what you want."

"It's not that easy. If anyone's gonna take this book seriously, I need money to pay for an editor, a designer for a professional cover, a formatter." She taps a finger as she ticks off each item.

"What if," Reina says, "and just hear me out. What if you could have a wish? Like anything you wanted. Would you wish to be a famous author?"

"Definitely!" Kali answers in a rush of excitement. "It wouldn't even feel like work if I could spend my days writing." She peers out the window, allowing the daydream to gel in her mind.

"Well, then I guess we'll just have to manifest it," Reina says with a blazing smile. Both are quiet for the rest of the drive as they imagine what their lives would be like if they had the freedom to do anything.

When the GPS announces that they're nearing their destination, Reina veers off the highway and follows a dusty road that winds around a mountain. At the end of the road, she parks and they hop out of the car.

"All right, so where are we headed?" Kali asks, pulling her auburn hair into a ponytail.

"Just over that ravine." Reina points in the distance. "Should take us about an hour but what's waiting for us on the other side of it will totally be worth it."

"Is it two single guys?" Kali laughs.

"Better!" Reina says as a sly grin passes over her face.

"Two rich single guys in search of a couple of hot chicks to spoil?" Kali's eyebrows jump in anticipation.

"Even better." Reina winks.

"Okay, now I know you're full of it because nothing can beat that." Kali rolls her eyes.

The conversation fades as they navigate up the rocky incline. Thin trees, sprawling ferns and patches of wild grass riddle the slope. Sweat dampens their hair as they trudge onward. Both suck in ragged breaths as they traverse the strenuous path. When they reach about three quarters of the way to the top, Reina stops and digs into her backpack. She pulls out a pair of binoculars. Holding them up to her eyes, she turns her head, tracking along the side of the mountain. After a few seconds, she freezes. Pointing to their right, she declares, "There. That's where we're headed."

In the distance, an opening protrudes from the side of the mountain, like a gaping mouth – a clear landmark of their entry point. With their target in sight, a renewed sense of purpose drives them to move faster, dodging gnarled branches and spindly twigs that stretch from trees and bushes along the rugged path.

As they near, a rustic sign with sharp, splintered edges stands just outside the opening. A few carved words confirm they're in the right place: Welcome to Ashveil Cavern, then in smaller letters right below it: Enter at your own risk.

The friends share an eager smile before reaching into their backpacks and fishing out flashlights.

"Now, we explore!" Kali declares, charging inside the veil of darkness.

Sweeping their beams of light across the mighty rock formation, they're both drawn to a bulge on the left side. Worn bricks, probably once a deep red, are faded to a dusty rose, their mortar crumbling in small piles on the ground. The well sits, rounded, jutting from the wall, as wide as a crop silo but not nearly as tall. It's sunken into the ground and completely open. They peer into the darkness below but it seems to be an empty hole with no end. Both women shiver as a chill dances across their skin. Twig-like vines hang from the crevice where the wall meets the jagged, arched ceiling.

Reina spots a narrow gap among the sea of green dangling along the wall. She weaves her fingers between the growth and splits it open wider, coughing when the sudden movement releases dust particles into the air.

"Look! A sign!" she squeals, pointing at a cracked, brittle rectangle carved from wood.

Kali sneezes. "Geez, it's dusty. Does anyone actually ever come here? Or just the spiders that call this place home?"

She brushes the cobwebs aside and they both read in silence. Primitive letters are scrawled into the ancient board.

Into the well, goes yer token
A small price to fix what is broken
Make yer wish, then trust in fate
It won't be long that ye shall wait
Time must pass before ye return
One wish a day is all ye may earn

"That's so cool," Kali mutters. She nudges her friend. "But just one wish after that hike? Is this some scheme to get us to keep coming back and dropping money in?"

"We won't need to come back!" Reina announces, digging into her pocket and holding up two quarters. She hands one to Kali. "Let's make our wish and then go have lunch so we can plan exactly what we'll do when our wishes come true!"

"Okay, you go first," Kali says, chewing on her fingernail. "You obviously had time to think about this since you planned the trip."

"Easy enough," Reina says as she dangles the quarter above the opening, a giant maw awaiting its payment. As her fingers release the coin, she leans toward the emptiness and calls out, "I want to be rich. Like, never-have-to-work-one-more-day-of-my-life kind of rich!" Her words echo in the void.

Kali wraps her arms around herself as another chill sweeps over her. Reina nods and, with a flourish, sidesteps around Kali so she can take a turn.

"I'm gonna wish for the time to finish my novel! If work wasn't so crazy, I could do it, and be one step closer to my dream!" Kali says.

"Why not just cut to the chase and wish that you were a bestselling author? Like right now?" Reina questions, as if she shouldn't even have to ask.

"I want to be a bestseller because people actually love my books, not because some mythical force makes it happen!" Kali shrugs. "Besides, if my book bombs, we'll just come back here and make some new wishes!"

"Now you're thinking!" Reina nods approvingly.

As Kali leans over the opening and calls out her wish, another sign buried beneath the foliage catches Reina's eyes. She wanders toward it and pulls the vines apart, sucking in a breath when the words come into focus.

> *Drop a coin and words in the hole*
> *Get what ye want but the cost is yer soul*

"Kali, come look at this." Reina's voice cracks as she points to the sign.

"What the . . . ?" Kali shakes her head. "This must be some kind of joke."

"Yeah, a joke," Reina agrees, nervously. "It's probably here to fit the mood."

The friends share a wary glance before Kali says, "Let's get out of here. I'm hungry!"

Twenty minutes after reaching the car, they find a local diner. As they wait for their greasy cheeseburgers and french fries, Kali grabs her phone and types Ashveil Caverns into a search engine. Her blood runs cold as she scrolls through article after article of people who claim the wishing well brought them tragedy.

"Reina, did you research this wishing well at all?" Kali asks, glancing up from the screen.

"I saw something about it on TikTok," Reina says, sipping her soda. "I thought it sounded cool and since we're not that far from it . . ."

"Well, I just looked it up and found some crazy stuff people say about it." Kali stares at her phone, scrolling as she explains. "Back in the 1960s, a woman jokingly wished her family appreciated her. Two days later they were in a car accident. They all survived but she was the only one not seriously injured. She became their caregiver, they were all dependent on her, until she lost her mind. I guess the stress got to be too much. She ended up in a psychiatric ward. Her husband and daughters had to go into assisted living."

The waitress arrives and plops their order on the table. The chipped white plates hold a mound of golden fries nestled beside a thick burger peeking out from beneath a sesame seed bun.

"That sounds made up, you can't trust everything you read on the internet," Reina says, dumping salt on her fries.

"Here's another one," Kali says, her face visibly pale. "About three years ago some guy wished to find the love of his life. It happened, kind of a love-at-first-sight thing. Months later he finds out she's a serial killer. Actually, he didn't find out, the police did, when they found his body!"

They fall into a distracted silence as fear and regret overtake disbelief. Both nearly jump out of the booth when the waitress reappears, asking if they need anything. As her cheeks flush, Kali shakes her head no. Both women pick at their food, the uncertainty of what happened weighing on them, eroding their appetites. After paying the check, they return to the car and head home, both lost in their thoughts.

"It'll all be fine," Reina says after a few minutes. "That stuff you found, they were just a few weird cases. Those people may have done things they didn't even realize they were doing that contributed to their problems."

"Yeah, you're right," Kali agrees. It feels better than considering what fate may await them.

The next morning, Kali storms out of her boss' office. She turns the corner to her desk only to find that her framed photos, water bottles, mug and tubes of lip balm and hand lotion are already boxed up. How nice, she thinks, while I'm distracted getting laid off, some HR lackey gathers all my stuff as if they can just erase me entirely. Kali channels every ounce of energy into holding back the tears stinging her eyes.

As her gaze sweeps across the cubicle one last time, a security guard announces himself and loads the packed boxes onto a cart. Her stomach twists in a knot of anxiety as she leads the guard to her car. She doesn't thank him for loading her meager belongings into the trunk. He wishes her well and turns back toward the building, clearly eager to get back to work.

Twisting the key in the ignition, Kali can't start the car fast enough. She speeds out of the parking lot, allowing the unshed tears to spill freely. Her drive home is blurry but thankfully there isn't much traffic. Most people are probably at work right now, she thinks wistfully.

When she reaches her apartment complex, she pulls the car into a parking space, cuts the engine and barrels to her front door. She'll have plenty of time to unpack the boxes later. All she cares about is retreating to her safe space, her protective bubble from the rest of the world.

After a bout of ugly crying, Kali picks up her phone and dials Reina. Her friend's voice on the other end is barely recognizable.

"Oh Kali." Reina pauses and sniffles. "Remember how my mom and dad . . . they went on that anniversary trip?"

"Yeah," Kali says, wondering how this is relevant to anything.

"The plane crashed." Reina's words are a whisper – a strained, forced admission. Her pain is palpable through the phone.

"No," Kali mutters, afraid of what she'll hear next.

"No survivors." Reina sobs on the other end.

"I'm coming over," Kali says, grabbing her car keys. "Just wait there for me."

Kali spends the next three hours trying to comfort her friend. She doesn't bring up her own bad news. Losing a job seems so trivial compared to losing parents. By the time she heads home, she's emotionally spent.

The next morning, Kali can't concentrate on anything. If this is supposed to be time spent writing her book, it's impossible. She's too stressed to think straight. Even looking for a new job feels daunting. By noon, she gives up and decides there's only one thing to do. She dials Reina but the call goes to voicemail immediately.

"Reina, we're going back to the well! I'll pick you up in ten minutes." She ends the call, storms through her apartment, grabbing a jacket and hiking boots. She jumps when her phone buzzes. It's a text from Reina.

Don't come. I'm not going back there. Ever.

Then a few seconds later:

Today I found out my parents had all kinds of investments they never told me about. Now it's all mine. I'm rich, Kali. I got what I wanted. This is all my fault and I'll never forgive myself.

Then I'll go myself, Kali thinks. *I'm not ready to give up yet.*

Hours later, Kali pulls into the same dirt lot that Reina parked in just a few days ago. She retraces their steps, winding through the narrow path, around branches and leaves, until she reaches the cavern's opening. She stomps inside, stopping when she reaches the well. The sight of it infuriates her. Taking a step toward the wall, she pounds a fist into it, cringing as a sharp jolt of pain bites her knuckles.

She bends down, rubbing her sore knuckles and squeezing her eyes shut. When she opens them, she notices a black sign hidden behind the vines. She brushes away the branches and leaves covering most of it. Bile rises in her throat as she reads the words. She knows it isn't a typo. It says *Wishing Hell.*

This damn thing is evil, she thinks. *All the stupid signs were hidden.*

She drops to her knees as hot tears spill down her cheeks. Thoughts race through her mind, each one a flawed solution that could never fix what has already happened. Digging into her pocket, she pulls out a quarter. Stepping up to the well, she drops it into the darkness.

"I wish this whole well would disappear forever!" she screams into the abyss. Resting her hands on the edges, she leans closer and repeats her wish, shouting even louder, releasing every molecule of rage burning within her.

She closes her eyes, wondering if she could have wished to go back in time, to the day Reina picked her up and brought her to this place. Hope blooms in her chest. Maybe she can prevent this from ever happening – it's worth a try. She can just tell Reina all about the wishing well and insist they go somewhere else. With a new resolve, she decides to come back tomorrow, when she can make another wish.

As she turns to leave, a deep rumbling stirs underground, unleashing sparks of energy beneath her feet. The air seems to grow heavy as panic sweeps through her. She stumbles as she tries to run. Before she reaches the cavern's gaping mouth, the well explodes into a fiery ball of fury, taking her with it to oblivion.

Acknowledgements

Thanks to all the readers who feed their souls by devouring page after page of someone's mindful ramblings. Authors spend a lot of time in their head and it is incredibly rewarding to bring a story to life. Even better is when someone enjoys reading it. Please consider leaving a rating or a review of *Whispers in the Dark* on Goodreads, Amazon and/or whatever retailer you may have purchased this book.

I'd also like to thank everyone who had a hand in preparing this book for its debut.

Diane Lesher, much appreciation for being an alpha reader for each story. You eagerly reviewed drafts when they still had notes and unfinished thoughts. Your feedback and willingness to bounce ideas back and forth helped solidify weak endings and vague references. And credit where it is due – Diane developed the concept for Family Secret. I simply ran with her ideas and named the main character after her!

Emily Angeline and Robin Asick, this is the eighth book you've beta read and at this point, I can't imagine writing a book without you! Your comments and suggestions highlighted sections that needed clarification so that the reader would "get" what was truly happening in the story. Thank you for being among the first sets of eyes on the manuscript.

Cheryl Lindbeck, I can't thank you enough for your enthusiasm and willingness to be an advanced reader copy reviewer. Your feedback motivates me to keep on typing! I'm so glad we connected!

Jen Blackwell, it has only been one year since we met and you've edited three of my books! Your input is invaluable and I know my manuscripts are in good hands when I send them your way. I look forward to our next project!

Scott, Landon and Aidan, thank you for always supporting me and for inspiring characters! So happy to be on this journey with you!

A. E. Faulkner was born and raised in Pennsylvania. When she's not lost in a book, she loves spending time with her family, which includes three humans, five rescue cats and a random number of foster kitties at any time.

One of her biggest fears is the repercussions we will face when nature can no longer tolerate human destruction. As such, she never tires of reading dystopian-themed tales.

Reach her at authoraefaulkner@gmail.com, visit www.authoraefaulkner.com or connect on social media: Facebook: @authaefaulkner Instagram: @authoraefaulkner TikTok: @authoraefaulkner

Also by A.E. Faulkner

The Nature's Fury series:
Darkness Falls (Book 1)
Anguish Unfolds (Book 2)
Devastation Erupts (Book 3)
Allegiance Unravels (Book 4)
Hope Emerges (Book 5)
Fate Collides (Short Story)

The Divided States series:
Upheaval (Book 1)
Uprising (Book 2)

The Spin (Gaia Awakens climate fiction anthology)
Culling Day (Gaia Awakens climate fiction anthology)
Hierarchy of Need (Nature Erupts climate fiction anthology)